MACK'S WITNESS

HEARTS & HEROES
BOOK 2

New York Times & USA Today
Bestselling Author

ELLE JAMES

Dedication

This book is dedicated to our military heroes past and present without whom we would not be the free nation we are.

A special thanks to Ireland for being such a fun place to visit. How lucky I feel to have run into a Travelers' wedding while there. And the castle bed and breakfast we stayed in was amazing, complete with a strong-willed proprietress. I hope to return soon to the Emerald Isle.

Chapter One

"Captain Mack, sniper on the south corner of the building ahead."

"Keep him in your sights, Gunny." Mack Magnus led one squad of his men toward the village from the south, while two other squads flanked the village from the west.

His point man had the best eye for spotting trouble. If not for Gunnery Sergeant Roy Tyler's eagle eye, they'd have lost a lot more men in the thirteen months since they'd deployed to Camp Leatherneck in the Helmand Province of Afghanistan.

This particular night they were operating on intel indicating a Taliban stronghold had been established in the small village nestled in the rocky hills. They'd spent the better part of the day maneuvering into position to storm the village at night when the enemy slept. The problem usually arose when the Taliban surrounded themselves by innocent civilians—women and children. They knew the American soldiers would balk at destroying an entire village if innocents were involved.

Cowards. This particular faction had recently lit a teenaged girl on fire and thrown her out of a speeding vehicle in front of a checkpoint to make an example of people who sided with anyone but the Taliban.

Embedded news reporters had a field day with the horrific images. No one could get to the girl without taking on live fire. By the time they reached her, she'd been burned to death, her screams something he'd never forget.

The squad halted outside the walled village and waited for the other squads to maneuver into place. Then one-by-one they slipped over the wall and dropped down on the other side, moving through the village to the largest building at the center where a Taliban meeting was said to be taking place that night.

Earlier, they'd watched from the nearby hillsides as vehicles entered the walled village, some were trucks loaded down with men in turbans, carrying Russian-made AK47s. Others were vans or cars. For a small village where most inhabitants didn't own a motorized car or truck, it was a lot of movement.

Mack had waited until dark before giving the order to move out.

Now inside the compound, they moved toward the target. Gunny climbed to the top of the building where the sniper sat and dispatched the man before he could fire a single round. The man must have fallen asleep at his post. He'd never do that again.

As the squads moved on the main building at the center of the village, the first shot rang out.

"Let's rumble," Mack said into his mic as the other squads moved into position. With his night vision goggles in place, he took the lead, moving building to building, firing on Taliban sentries.

Gunny dropped down from the sniper's position and joined Mack and the rest of the squad rushing the building.

Mack reached for a concussion grenade clipped to his

vest, pulled the pin, kicked in the door to the building and tossed the grenade inside.

He ducked to the side of the door and held his hands over his ears as did the others. The grenade went off with a muffled whomp. His feet vibrated beneath him and the wall he leaned on shook.

Then he moved into the building and stepped over the bodies of two men and gathered the guns they'd carried, handing them back to Gunny, who would quickly strip the bolts out of the weapons and slam the stock into the wall to break it against any future attempt at use against American forces.

The deeper he moved into the structure, the more he realized there were no other men but the original sentries.

"Got trouble on the south side of the village!" Someone shouted into his headset.

Sounds of rifle reports came to Mack through the thick walls. Mack pointed to the exit and shouted, "Go! Go! Go!"

As he emerged from the building, he nearly tripped over Lance Corporal Jenson lying on his side moaning, his hand clutching his thigh drenched in blood.

A bullet hit the building over Mack's right shoulder, dusting him in powder and pebbles from the stucco.

He dropped to his haunches and glanced up through his night vision goggles. On the top corner of the building down the street from where he crouched, he saw the green heat signature of a warm body and the bright flash of bullet rounds. Mack raised his rifle to his shoulder, held his breath and squeezed the trigger. The man on the roof tipped over and fell to the ground.

Mack shouted, "Gunny, stay here and help Jenson."

"Yes, sir." Gunny bent over the lance corporal, administering a quick field dressing and light tourniquet to slow the bleeding.

Mack moved through the maze of streets and walled yards, following the sound of rifle fire, hurrying to join the others.

As he rounded a corner, something dropped in front of him and rolled.

"Grenade!" he shouted and threw himself back around the corner, knocking into the rest of his squad.

A loud bang shook the earth.

"Sir." A slender hand shook his shoulder and a voice with a light Irish lilt said, "Sir, we've just landed at Dublin International Airport. Are ya all right?"

Mack blinked awake and sat up straighter, taking a moment to orient himself to his environment. "Dublin?"

"Yes, sir." The diminutive, older woman sitting beside him smiled. "You were having a wee bit of a bad dream."

Mack ran a hand down his face, wishing he'd had time to scrape the day's growth of beard off before heading straight for his brother's bachelor party. Hell, he'd like to have slept a day or two before the events. He'd pulled every string to fly out of Afghanistan a day earlier than the remainder of his unit re-deploying stateside.

"Are ya here on business or pleasure?" the woman asked as the plane taxied down the runway to the terminal.

He hadn't talked the entire trip, closing his

eyes as soon as the plane took off from Frankfurt. He'd arrived at Ramstein Air Force Base and made a mad dash to the international airport at Frankfurt, Germany, to catch his flight to Ireland. Exhausted and in need of rest, he'd leaned back in his seat and gone right to sleep. Now that he was in Ireland, he was expected to be awake and ready to celebrate Wyatt's wedding festivities.

Mack swallowed a groan. "I'm not here on business or pleasure. I'm here for my brother's wedding."

"A wedding, is it?" The woman smiled and patted his hand on the armrest. "A fine place for a wedding. There's no better place in the world than the Emerald Isle. Their wedding will be truly blessed."

"Sure." Mack didn't have a whole lot of faith in wedded bliss lasting. The odds of most marriages ending in divorce were too high for him to take the leap. He couldn't believe his brother was willing to commit himself to the institution. Mack wondered if he'd knocked her up and felt obligated to marry her. Having been on maneuvers for the past few months, he hadn't had time to talk with Wyatt about his engagement or the upcoming wedding.

Hell, none of his brothers had met the woman. She might not even be right for Wyatt. With him in the army, the chances of this marriage lasting were even slimmer. All the more reason for Mack to make the effort to get there before the wedding. He needed to talk to Wyatt and remind him it wasn't too late to call it off.

"Your brother is a lucky man to have found love in Ireland."

"He didn't actually find his fiancée in Ireland. They met in San Antonio, Texas, in the U.S. I don't know why they decided to have the wedding in Ireland. I think she has relatives here."

"The wedding is in Dublin?"

"As far as I know."

"I met me husband in Dublin when I was a young lass. He swept me off my feet and carried me away to a castle." She stared out at the terminal as the plane rolled to a stop at the gate. "If you have the opportunity to visit Cahir, please, come stay with me in my castle. Me husband and I converted it to a bed-and-breakfast to help with the expense of upkeep. Now that me husband is gone, I manage it mostly by meself. Castle O'Leary B-and-B is its name."

"Thanks, but I think we'll be staying in Dublin the entire time, then I'm headed back to the States." Ah, the States. He planned on taking the full four weeks off, relaxing somewhere on a beach in California near the Marine base. He might even fly out to Texas to his little stretch of heaven in the hill country. The hundred acres of scrub he'd purchased with his signing bonus.

The woman held out her hand. "Me name's Katherine O'Leary, but me friends all call me Kate." She handed him a business card. "If ya ever find yerself in need of a place to stay in Ireland, come to Castle O'Leary. I serve a fine Irish breakfast each morning."

To be nice to the woman, Mack took her card and slipped it into his wallet as the seatbelt sign blinked off. He stood, grabbed his backpack from the overhead bin and stepped out of the way for Kate to stand in the aisle as they waited for the doors to open and the flight to offload.

"Is someone meetin' ya here, or will ya be takin' the train into the city?"

"I'm supposed to have a ride."

"A ride, is it?" She giggled. "Just so you know, in Ireland a ride means sex. It's a lift you'll be wantin'. Well, then, Dia dhuit." Kate smiled and translated. "That's Gaelic for God be with you."

"Thank you," Mack said, not certain how to respond to the older woman who'd just set him straight on sex. "And Dee a dwaht to you," he added awkwardly.

The door opened to the jetway and passengers shuffled out like cattle in a chute. Mack couldn't wait to get his feet on solid earth and a beer in his hand. After thirteen months in an alcohol-free combat zone, he was ready to relax.

As Kate, an Irish national, went one way, Mack joined the long line of foreigners waiting their turn to process through customs. After another forty minutes, he was finally headed toward the door marked Ground Transportation. If his ride—he chuckled—lift wasn't there, he'd hire a rental car and get himself to the hotel.

That's when he remembered...he didn't know what hotel they were staying at. The e-mail he'd gotten from Wyatt had been vague. Fiona's cousin would be waiting for him near the exit for his terminal.

Hell, he'd been in such a hurry to catch his flights he hadn't stopped to ask who Fiona's cousin was or what he looked like. In a terminal full of people coming and going, he could spend a lot of time searching for the cousin.

He stood staring through the exit door and looking back over his shoulder in case he'd walked by the cousin and didn't know it. He felt stupid for not asking for a name or description.

A man walked by carrying a sign with a name on it. Mack started to follow him, until he turned and Mack could read the sign. O'Brien.

He resumed his position near the exit and waited, tired, a little on the grumpy side and ready for that beer.

A woman stepped into the terminal wearing a white, calf-length trench coat, sunglasses and a scarf over her hair. The little bit of legs Mack could see below the coat were trim, smooth, well-defined and gorgeous. He couldn't tell what color hair was beneath the scarf, nor the color of her eyes beneath the sunglasses. The manner in which she carried herself was enough to make Mack look twice. She could be a runway model the way she strode across the floor, one foot in front of the other, the trench coat in no way disguising her tiny waist and slim hips.

A woman like that had to be high-maintenance and completely full of herself, and most likely boring in bed. Basically, an ice princess. Though she was wonderful eye-candy, Mack was not the least interested.

He glanced back at the entrance, wondering when his lift would show up, starting to think he might have to find his own way there.

"Excuse me, sir," a lilting Irish voice said. "What is yer name?"

Mack's insides tightened, and he turned to face the woman with the voice that tugged at something primal.

The ice princess stood in front of him, her full, lush red lips pressed into a thin line. Then she snapped her fingers in his face. "Are you addled?"

"Addled?"

"Do you not speak English?" She stood so close Mack could see several wisps of deep auburn hair sneaking out from beneath the scarf.

He wanted to reach out and yank the scarf from her head and let the dark red hair free. "Yes, I speak English."

"American, eh?" The woman drew herself up on her heels almost but not quite eye-to-eye with him. "Perhaps you could help me. I'm looking for an American named Mack Magnus."

So she was his ride...er, lift. A thrill of annoyance and desire speared through him. Her attitude was beginning to get under his skin along with the desire to pull her into his arms and kiss the lush red lips until he smudged her lipstick.

"Silly name, if you ask me." The ice princess glanced around and back to him, her head dipping as if she was looking him over from head to toe. "You sort of fit the description I was given, but I assumed he'd be a bit more…"

"Handsome?" Mack fought the smile pulling at his lips.

Her brows lifted above the rims of her sunglasses. "The word I was looking for was intelligent."

Mack chuckled. "It just so happens I know Mack Magnus."

"You do? Could you point him out for me?" Again, she looked around at the crowd of people moving in and out of the terminal.

"I could…on one condition."

Her brows disappeared below the edge of the big sunglasses. "Condition?"

He nodded. "Show me your eyes."

Her lips pursed, making Mack want to kiss them even more. "And why should I show you my eyes?"

"I'm curious as to what color they are." He reached up to touch the scarf covering her hair. "Red hair should have green eyes."

She snorted. "My eyes have nothing to do with you or my finding Mr. Magnus."

"I guess you don't want to find this Magnus person." He nodded toward the rush of people. "Go on. Find him yourself."

The woman squared her shoulders and performed an elegant spin worthy of a runway model and marched away.

After a full two minutes of weaving in and out

of the crowds gathered around the baggage carousels, she returned.

"Fine. I'll show you my eyes if you'll point out Mack Magnus. Only briefly, because I don't normally take off my sunglasses in public." She turned her head left then right, before removing the sunglasses. "There. Are you happy?" She blinked up at him, her eyes a smoky shade of blue that contrasted brilliantly with her deep auburn hair.

"Beautiful," he said, mesmerized by them.

For a long moment she stared back, the blue of her eyes deepening. Her tongue darted out to swipe a glistening path across her lips and she pressed the hand holding her glasses to her chest. "Are you always this bold?" she whispered.

"Always."

She caught her bottom lip between her teeth and her gazed lowered to his mouth.

He could swear he'd seen those eyes somewhere. Recently. His brows drew together as he tried to remember. "Do I know you?"

She sighed and slid the glasses back on her face. "No. Surely, had I met you before now, I'd remember you for the attractive, yet unfortunately rude and obnoxious, American you are. Now, please point to Mr. Magnus. I have much to do and collecting him is cutting into my time."

"Then you'll be happy to know you've been talking to the man with the silly name all along." He swept a low bow in front of her. "I'm Mack Magnus."

"Jazus, Mary and Joseph." Her smooth tones slipped into an earthier Irish accent and she planted her hands on her hips. "Why didn't you say so in the first place?"

"I would have, but you were on a tear to be as rude and obnoxious as you claimed I was being."

"Jeekers, come with me." She spun on her heels and tripped over Mack's backpack where he'd dropped it on the floor.

He reached out, snagged her hand and yanked her into his arms to keep her from falling flat on her face. The scarf slipped from her head and the sunglasses fell from her face. Her hair tumbled about her shoulders in wild disarray.

Fourteen months in the desert was a long time to go without holding a woman in his arms, a long time without the taste of a woman, without the feel of the soft curves of her body…Mack groaned. The urge to kiss her won and he lowered his lips to hers, claiming them in a searing kiss.

Deirdre Darcy gasped and Mack's tongue swept through the gap between her teeth to caress hers in a long slow glide of wet, sensuous heat. Her fingers curled into his shirt, dragging him closer when she should have pushed the bloody bastard away. Damn him for being so good-looking and cocksure.

When she'd entered the airport, her gaze had found him in an instant. Though she knew plenty of beautiful men through her experiences as a model, she hadn't met one with as much ruggedly masculine charisma as Mack.

As he lifted his lips from hers, he whispered, "Definitely beautiful."

Her heart fluttered and she swayed toward him, wanting a replay of the kiss, not nearly satisfied with just one.

Lights flashed and the click of cameras surrounded them.

"What the hell?" Mack straightened, setting her upright on her feet.

"Feckin' papparazi." Deirdre lifted her scarf up over her hair and snatched her sunglasses from where they'd caught on her sleeve, slipping them over her eyes. "If you want a lift, come with me now."

Before he could take a step toward the door, a woman shoved a microphone in his face. "Sir, are you Deirdre Darcy's lover?"

"I don't know what you're talking about." He pushed the microphone away from his face and matched Deirdre's steps as she exited the terminal.

A man carrying a camera jumped in front of Deirdre, blocking her path. "Ms. Darcy, we understand you're attending a wedding this weekend. Is it yours? Is this man your fiancé?" He snapped several pictures, the flash blinking again and again.

Glad for her sunglasses, Deirdre ignored the question and started around the man. He moved to the side, blocking her yet again. This was exactly the kind of situation she'd hoped to avoid and was dead tired of dealing with.

Mack stepped up beside her and pushed himself between the man with the camera and Deirdre, gripping her elbow in his massive paw. "You're blocking the lady's path."

Much larger than the reporter, Mack towered over him, glaring down his nose like an angry bull.

The man's eyes widened and he stepped aside.

Deirdre marched to the parking garage where she'd left her car, her lips twitching at the way her path cleared with the big American by her side. She could get used to this. Perhaps she should hire a bodyguard when she went out in public. A big one with rock-hard muscles and hands that could hold her like she was lighter than a feather. A guard who could kiss like the feckin' devil himself.

She stumbled. If not for Mack's hand on her arm, she'd have gone headfirst into the side of her car. Straightening, she stared up into Mack's deep-blue eyes and gulped. She swallowed hard before she could get words past her vocal chords. "You can store your bag in the boot." Without waiting for his response, she clicked the button releasing the lock on the lid of the boot.

Mack let go of her arm. "Are you okay?"

"I'll be better once we're out of here." She shook free of his grip, walked around to the right side of the vehicle and slid behind the steering wheel.

Once Mack had stowed his bag and slid into the passenger seat, Deirdre eased the shift into reverse and backed out of the parking space.

"Deirdre Darcy." Mack tapped his finger to

his chin and finally shook his head. "Name rings a bell, but I've been too long in the sandbox to remember why. Suppose you enlighten me."

"Sandbox?"

"Afghanistan."

She knew Wyatt's brothers were in the military, but she hadn't stopped to think of where. That they'd been in hostile countries, possibly being shot at, hadn't crossed her mind. Suddenly her status as an internationally known public figure seemed unimportant to the point of trivial. "I guess you could say I'm a celebrity in Ireland."

Once they were out of the parking garage, she pushed the scarf off her head, leaving her sunglasses in place, not ready to reveal her thoughts through her eyes. Every photographer she'd ever worked with had told her that her eyes were the windows to her soul. Every emotion she felt was revealed. For some reason, she didn't want her every thought on display for the handsome man in the seat next to her to see. He was too confident, cocky and annoying by far. And his kiss had left her confused and, for the first time in a decade, needy.

"Celebrity?" He turned toward her. "Actress? Newscaster? No, don't tell me. Weathergirl?"

Deirdre frowned. "None of those." She nodded toward a billboard sign at the side of the highway. "See that sign?"

Mack's glance darted to the sign as they drove past.

In larger-than-life size and brilliant contrasts

of dark and light was a woman in a white evening gown with a plunging neckline. She stood in front of a shiny black Mercedes, her deep auburn hair twisted up in an elegant chignon at the back of her head.

Deirdre waited for recognition to dawn.

"Sorry, what was it you wanted me to see? Great car, by the way."

"The woman on the sign. Jazus, Mary and Joseph, you are thick."

"She wasn't bad." Mack shrugged. "A little too highbrow for me."

"You dunce! That's me. Deirdre Darcy. I'm an international model in high demand by every major advertising company in the global market." She glanced at him. He really had no clue who she was. "Oh, that's right, you've been rolling around in the sand for how long?"

"Thirteen months." He winked at her. "I knew it was you. Are you on very many billboards?"

"I've been modeling for nearly a decade."

"Sorry. I'm not much into high fashion. I'm a blue jeans and T-shirt kind of guy when I'm not in uniform."

Why she was letting his sad lack of recognition get to her, she didn't know. Most days she wished for the solitude and anonymity of one who hadn't made a living by having her face plastered over every billboard or television commercial. But Mack's complete disregard for her... Her what?

Self-importance? Her foot left the accelerator as she contemplated her thought. Mack didn't give a kiss of the Blarney Stone for her career or her superstar status. Once she got past her own arrogance, she could appreciate his open honesty. Although he'd been a bit too honest. He'd called her obnoxious. She'd never been obnoxious a day in her life.

Okay, sometimes her red hair got her into trouble. She shook her head to clear her musings. "Which one of Wyatt's brothers are you?"

"I'm the older brother. The other two are younger."

"And all of you are in the U.S. military?"

"We are." He smiled, staring straight ahead as if revisiting a good memory. "Not all of us are in the same branch of the military. Wyatt joined the Army Special Forces. I'm in the Marines. Ronin is a SEAL and Sam is an Army helicopter pilot."

"Are there any more of you?"

"We have a sister. She should be on her way here."

"Is she also in the military?"

"No, she chose to join the U.S. Foreign Services. She works at the embassy in the Ukraine. Much to our father's disappointment."

"Why?"

"She's the baby he always tried to protect. And you know the troubles they're having in Russia now."

Deirdre nodded. "I can understand his hesitation."

"Abby has always had a stubborn streak." Mack smiled. "But she loves her job and she's good at it."

When he talked about his little sister, Mack's smile deepened and he looked more relaxed, less stressed. Positively gorgeous. And gorgeous usually meant one thing. Trouble. "I'm sure if your sister got into trouble, her big brothers would come bail her out, right?"

"Damn right. Speaking of parents...have mine arrived?"

"They settled into the hotel and are getting some rest after their long flight from the States."

"Good. I know Mom will love being here. She always wanted to come to Ireland."

As Deirdre drove through the streets of Dublin, she reflected on how close the Magnus family seemed. A twinge of regret tugged at her. In her global travels following her chosen career, she'd lost the closeness she'd grown up with. The camaraderie of a close-knit Irish family. Sure, she got together on occasion with the rest of her large, extended family, but she didn't have that connection they all seemed to have. Perhaps she'd been away too long.

Fiona had been the one cousin she'd kept in touch with most and she'd grown up in America. Fiona's mother was Irish, Deirdre's aunt, her father had been in the military. She'd been like Deirdre, constantly on the move, never content to stay in one place. When Fiona had informed her she wanted her to be her maid of honor at her wedding in Dublin, Deirdre couldn't say no.

What she hadn't counted on was how much work was involved in the maid of honor position. Though had she known, she still would have accepted. Fiona was a wonderful woman who deserved every happiness.

A little twinge of something akin to envy tweaked beneath the surface as Deirdre made arrangements for the informal wedding at a very old church a friend of the family was able to secure on short notice for the event.

Who knew ordering flowers and arranging for a pianist would spark such a strong tug of longing in herself and a deepening dissatisfaction with her career and the direction her life was heading?

Fiona had been a career woman set in her independent ways when she'd met and fallen in love with Wyatt Magnus. A whirlwind of a romance and three months after they'd met they were scheduled to marry in Ireland and honeymoon in Crete.

Deirdre sighed. Why did some people make falling in love appear so easy? One minute you're happily pursuing your career, the next you're falling all over yourself to please your man.

Fiona's Magnus brother must be as handsome and appealing as the one in Deirdre's car. In that case, Deirdre could understand Fiona wanting to stake her claim before another woman discovered her goldmine of a catch.

"We're staying at the Fitzpatrick Hotel, a four-star hotel close to the church. I believe you'll be comfortable there."

"Sweetheart, I could be comfortable on a stone floor as long as the temperatures don't get above one hundred, no one is shooting at me and sand isn't getting stuck in those really hard to reach cracks. For your information, if we ever go beyond that kiss back there, I can promise you that we won't be making love on a beach. I've had enough sand in my shorts to last a lifetime."

Deirdre's pulse quickened at an image of herself making love with the American on a sandy beach, warm waves washing over their naked bodies. She quickly squelched the image and lifted her chin. "I'll keep that in mind. But for the record, we will never hook up or make love. You're not my type."

He chuckled. The deep rumble in his chest setting her heart to racing. "And what type is that?" he asked.

"I don't know what it is, but I'll make sure you're the first to know when I do."

"Ah, a woman who doesn't know what she wants. Perhaps you haven't been with a man who can show you exactly what it is you need."

She shot him a surprised look. "Cocky much, Yank?"

He shrugged. "Just saying, you haven't been with a real man if you still don't know what you want in the way of sex."

She snorted. "Oh dear, and I suppose you would be the expert to show me?"

"I didn't say that."

"Good. Because I'd have to call you an arrogant braggart."

"I wouldn't want you to sink to name-calling." He grinned and leaned back in the seat. "You have an international image to uphold. Besides, I'm not into high-maintenance women, and you, sweetheart, have high-maintenance written all over you."

She relaxed against her seat, a smile lifting her lips. "You say that like high-maintenance is a bad thing."

"That's right. I'm just here for the weekend and then I'm on to my much-deserved vacation. I only have time and energy enough for a quick fling with the low-maintenance type. No strings attached."

And in a flash, her heartbeat jumped at the American's suggestion of a fling. Not that he wanted one with her. She was high-maintenance, and he wasn't going to be around for long. Then he'd be off to the States for a vacation then back to some far corner of the world to be shot at or worse.

However, if she wanted to have an affair with a gorgeous man, she'd be hard-pressed to find a physical specimen as gorgeous as Mack. It had been over a year since she'd been with a man, and he'd been less than a gentleman, wanting only to be with her because of her status in the fashion industry. How refreshing would it be to make love to a man who only wanted a willing woman, not a leg up in his business?

The weekend was looking to be more interesting by the minute. As with most celebrations in Ireland, the pre-wedding and wedding activities promised to be entertaining. With a roomful of Magnus brothers, it could be even more entertaining.

"As the best man, am I required to do anything besides stand with my brother and make the first toast to the happily married couple?"

"Seriously?" She glanced his way. "You're the best man. You're supposed to be in charge of the bachelor party, not just going there for a drink."

Mack frowned and sat up. "I forgot about that part. I had really hoped to have a drink and call it a night."

"Hard to believe," Deirdre muttered.

"Seriously, how hard can it be? You know a stripper I can hire on short notice?"

"I do not!" Deirdre exclaimed.

"Well, damn. I'm already falling down on the job. What about a bar where we can go get shit-faced drunk?"

"You won't be pissin' the night away on the eve of my cousin's wedding."

"It's tradition. My brother needs to celebrate his last night as a bachelor."

"And my cousin doesn't need to celebrate her last night as a single woman?"

"Absolutely."

"I'll be sure to line up a stripper for her."

"I thought you didn't know any strippers."

"I only know the male strippers. I assumed

you meant female."

He shot a sideways glance her way and winked. "Like I said, you are high-maintenance."

Her belly clenched at that wink and her fingers tightened on the steering wheel. The man had a way of making her body hum with just a look. Feckin' American. "For your information, I've already arranged for the bachelor and bachelorette parties to be held at the Donegal, a small pub in the heart of Dublin. We will have the place to ourselves."

"That won't do at all. The bride and groom need to celebrate separately."

"And they will. The women will be in the back room of the bar and the men will be in the front. Quite separate."

He glanced her way. "You'll be there?"

She lifted her chin. "I'm the maid of honor. I have to be there for my cousin."

"Hmm." His gaze shifted forward. "Save a dance for me, will ya?"

"There'll be little burnin' up the tiles tonight."

"There will be if there's music." He gave her a sexy smile. "Save the dance."

Her knuckles turning white on the steering wheel, she pulled in front of the hotel where they had booked a quarter of the rooms for members of the wedding party. "The pub is within walkin' distance, a block and a half in that direction." She pointed as she turned off the engine and pulled the keys from the ignition. "You'll have just enough time for a shower and to change clothes."

"Is there a dress code?"

She glanced across at him, loving the way he looked in denim. "Something better than jeans will do. Meet me in the lobby in one hour and we'll walk to the pub together. I'd like to be there before the rest of the wedding party to make certain everything is in place."

"Are you sure you weren't a drill sergeant in a previous life?"

"No, but I have four younger cousins I used to keep after school." She slid out of the vehicle, hit the button to unlock the boot and handed the keys to a uniformed valet. She waited for Mack to gather his bag and join her on the sidewalk, before she continued. "I know how to handle bold little boys."

Mack leaned close to her, his lips near her ear. "Just so you know. I'm not a little boy." He kissed the side of her throat, captured the back of her neck and kissed her full on the lips before straightening.

Her heart thundering against her ribs, Deirdre couldn't force a word past her vocal cords. The man was entirely too bold...and big...and sexy as hell.

Then he winked and her knees wobbled.

"See you in an hour," he promised.

Chapter Two

Mack checked into his room and threw his backpack onto the bed. When he'd gotten off the airplane with his internal clock jacked up from the time changes, he'd been more concerned about catching some more Z's as soon as he reached his room.

If not for the chance to spar with the pretty international model, he'd call foul and indulge in that siesta he so badly needed. But the beautiful redhead was too tempting to leave standing alone in the lobby for long. One of his brothers would likely bump into her and hit on her.

Mack pulled his trousers out of his pack and shook out a white button-up dress shirt. Other than the jeans he wore, a couple of pullover shirts and a casual blazer, he hadn't packed much. Marines didn't take anything but uniforms when they deployed. For the purpose of coming to the wedding, he'd had some of his civilian clothing mailed to him from stateside. As soon as he'd disembarked off the military aircraft at Ramstein, he'd ditched his desert camouflage uniform. He'd changed into the jeans, pullover polo shirt and jacket before taking a train to Frankfurt where he'd flown out on a commercial flight to Ireland.

The marine in him refused to allow himself to

show up at the party in wrinkled clothing. He pulled the ironing board out of the closet and plugged in the iron before hopping into the shower. A few minutes later he emerged, refreshed and feeling almost human with every trace of sand completely erased from his body.

A quick run over his clothes with the iron removed the wrinkles and he dressed in black trousers, the white shirt and the dress shoes he'd pair with the tux Wyatt had rented for him to wear to the wedding.

When he was fully clad, he slipped on the blazer, shoved his wallet into his pocket and stepped out into the hallway, determined to find the brothers he hadn't seen in over a year, then the redhead.

Avoiding the elevator, Mack found the stairs and hurried down to the lobby and the reception desk to ask about Wyatt, Ronin and Sam. Abby was due in later that night.

The lobby was crowded with a startling array of characters. Men strutted across the tile floor with dark hair, heavy brows and tattoos on their wrists and knuckles. Dressed in black suits and dark, narrow neckties, they were bulky men who looked like they bench-pressed automobiles for fun. Behind them paraded women in over-the-top, red, white, teal and purple Cinderella dresses, with wide skirts of tulle and taffeta. Low-cut necklines exposed vast amounts of bosoms and cutouts on the sides of the dresses displayed midriffs. Their makeup was garish and their hair piled high, cascading down in ringlets. Even the little girls wore the big dresses and high heels, with thick makeup and hairstyles matching the adults. The lobby looked like the set of one of the reality TV shows of a trailer trash family striking it rich.

Mack waded through the throng of people to the reception desk where a pretty young woman stood behind the counter. "Might I help ya?" she asked in that lyrical Irish accent.

"What's going on?" Mack tipped his head toward the melee.

The woman grinned. "There's a Travelers' weddin' goin' on in the main ballroom."

Mack frowned. "Travelers?"

"The Irish version of gypsies." She glanced toward one of the women whose large breasts looked to be about to explode from the dress. "Quite fanciful, don't you think?"

"That's one way of putting it."

The receptionist gave her full attention to Mack. "How might I help you?"

"I'm looking for the Magnus brothers."

"Mack? Is that you?" a voice said behind him.

He turned to find all three of his brothers and his parents grinning at him. They converged in a backslapping, laughing, hugging huddle.

Mack hugged his mother and shook hands with his father and then hugged him.

"Oh, honey, you look thin," his mother said. "Don't they feed you boys in the marines?"

Mack laughed. "Yes, Mom, they do."

"It's good to see you, son," his father said.

"Your mother and I need to check on the arrangements for the wedding tomorrow. You boys go, have a good time."

"Just not too good," his mother warned with a stern frown, softened by a smile.

"We'll be careful," Mack promised.

Once his parents had gone, Mack turned to his brothers.

"You old son-of-a-bitch." Wyatt engulfed him in a bear hug. "How's the corps treating you?"

"Good. Fortunately we were wrapping up a tour when you decided to tie the knot."

Wyatt grinned. "Can you believe it? I'm getting married."

Ronin clapped a hand against Wyatt's back. "We all thought for sure Mack would be the first to cave."

Mack shook his head. "Not me. I'm married to the corps."

"Yeah, no offense, but the corps doesn't make a great bedfellow," Wyatt said. "In fact, I'm sure they aren't too good at providing decent beds, am I right?"

"Beats the hell out of what the Army gives you." Mack stuck out a hand, clasped Ronin's and pulled him into a hug. "Good to see you. Crashed any helicopters lately?"

Ronin laughed. "Sorry to report, no crashes."

"Life a little on the boring side with the 160th Night Stalkers?" Mack asked.

His pilot brother nodded. "Due for another rotation soon, if they don't recall all our troops as planned."

"Don't unpack your bags yet." Mack clapped a hand on Ronin's shoulder. "Things are still unstable over there. I doubt we'll pull out yet."

"Thanks for the heads up."

"What about you, little brother?" Mack shook hands with Sam and pulled him into a hug. "Been on any super-secret missions lately?"

"If I told you about them—"

"You'd have to kill me, right?" Mack chuckled. "Same ol', same ol' with the Navy SEALs."

"No, I'm doing something different this year."

"Oh yeah?"

"The wedding is just the beginning of my first-ever month off."

"Month?" Mack's brows rose. "What are you going to do for a whole month?"

Sam shrugged. "Thought I'd backpack through Europe."

"Don't you travel enough with the Navy?"

"Not like this." Sam's face split in a grin. "I want to go where people aren't shooting at me."

"What are you looking for? An easy day? I thought you SEALs went by the motto, the only easy day was yesterday."

"We do. But I've been on one mission after another. I could use some downtime."

"Sorry, brother." Wyatt patted Sam's back. "We have one more mission before you can take that break you so desperately need."

"So, what are we calling this mission?" Mack draped an arm across Wyatt's shoulder. "Something catchy, I hope."

"Operation: Get Wyatt Hitched?" Sam offered.

Mack snorted. "That's all you got?"

"Why not something like Operation: Ball and Chain?" Ronin proffered.

"Come on, guys." Wyatt checked his watch. "It's my wedding, not my funeral, and Fiona is great. Wait until you meet her. Even then, don't pass judgment. I'm the one marrying her, and I love her."

"A good thing too. I wouldn't wear a monkey suit for just anyone." Mack playfully punched Wyatt in the shoulder. "She better be worth it, brother."

Wyatt nodded. "She is. Speaking of Fiona, I wonder where she is." He glanced around the lobby at the women in bright costumes parading through. "Can you believe this circus?"

Mack laughed. "The receptionist said they're gypsies here for their own wedding."

Ronin elbowed Wyatt in the belly. "Is that the kind of dress Fiona's going to wear?" He pointed to a particular woman in a bright purple dress with yards and yards of fluffy fabric floating around her.

"I hope not," Wyatt responded.

Deirdre chose that moment to appear in the midst of the dazzling dresses and rhinestone-studded gowns. She wore a little black dress, her white coat and a cobalt-blue scarf draped over her arm, deep red hair flowing around her shoulders like a lion's mane. Compared to the Travelers, Deirdre was understated and elegant. Every step she took was like poetry in motion. And she walked straight toward Mack.

"Beautiful." His pulse rocketed and his groin tightened.

Wyatt chuckled. "I see you've met Fiona's cousin Deirdre."

"Holy shit, Mack," Ronin said, "introduce me."

Deirdre stopped beside Mack. "Ready?"

"I am. But first, my baby brothers want to meet you." Mack turned to Wyatt. "I take it you've met Wyatt?"

"I have. The man who stole my cousin's heart. Welcome to the family." Her eyes narrowed. "If you break Fiona's heart, I'll come for you."

"And hell knows no fury like an Irish woman after revenge?" Ronin stepped forward and held out his hand. "If you were my woman, I'd never break your heart."

Mack wanted to jump between his brother and Deirdre and tell him to back off. He took a step forward, but Deirdre's hand on his arm held him back.

Deirdre shook Ronin's hand. "I appreciate the sentiment. But my heart's not up for breakin'. Pleasure to meet you though."

"Ouch." Ronin pulled his hand back as if it had been burned. "If you change your mind…"

Her shoulders squared. "I won't change my

mind."

Sam pushed Ronin aside. "Out of the way, loser." He held out his hand to Deirdre and she took it. "I'm Sam. Do you have a date for tonight?"

"No." Deirdre pulled her fingers out of his and held her hand up. "And I don't want one. Nice to meet you, Sam." She turned to Mack. "If you're ready?"

Mack didn't bother to hide his smile. "Crash, Froggy, Wyatt, I'll see you shortly at the pub." He hooked Deirdre's arm and led her toward the door. He hadn't taken two steps when she stopped, stared down at the hand on her arm and back up at Mack with her brows cocked.

He released her arm and cringed. His brothers' laughter echoed over the Travelers' commotion as he followed Deirdre to the door.

She wove her way confidently through the steady stream of outlandishly attired wedding guests.

Mack had it half-right when he'd pegged her for an ice queen. If not for the way she'd responded to his kiss, he'd still think of her as such. But that kiss gave him hope she wasn't as frigid as she pretended to be.

"Are you and your brothers always so cocksure?" she asked.

"You have to be in our line of work. Who else would put themselves up for enemy target practice?"

"You have a point." Deirdre stepped through

the door of the hotel and out onto the sidewalk.

Mack followed, enjoying the way her bottom swayed in the figure-hugging black dress. Once outside, she shivered.

"You'll need that coat." He took it from her hands and held it for her while she slipped her arms into sleeves. "By the way, you look great." He rested his hands on her shoulders longer than he should, the scent of her hair doing funny things to his insides. He had the urge to pull her into his arms, turn her around and kiss her like there was no tomorrow. While he hesitated, she stepped way.

Deirdre pulled the edges of her coat together and faced him. "You're not so bad yourself, Yank." Her gaze swept his length from the top of his head to his shiny black shoes.

Everywhere her gaze landed tingled, sending heated messages throughout his body to pool in his groin. If she continued to stare at him like that, he'd be forced to drag her against him and steal that kiss.

Drawing in a deep breath, he held out his arm. "We should be going."

"Yes, indeed, we should." She lifted her chin and turned, leading the way down the street. They walked to the next block and turned left. Streetlights lit the way and cars passed in a steady flow.

For a few minutes, Mack felt they could have been any couple strolling along the street, and he found himself liking it. Too much. He was only there for the weekend and he didn't believe in love or commitment. She wasn't in the market for a relationship, and she'd made herself pretty clear on that subject to him and his brothers.

Mack, ol' buddy, since when did you back down from a challenge?

Despite the cold, damp air, a fire warmed inside Deirdre as she walked beside Mack. Other than the kiss, the man had been a perfect gentleman, which was beginning to irritate her. When he'd helped her into her coat, she thought for sure he'd try to pinch another kiss. She'd been ready to give the Yank a good set down, but then he'd done nothing. No kiss, no embrace. Nothing. Jazus, what was wrong with him?

Her brows tugged together. Had he been disappointed by their earlier kiss?

Deirdre shook her head. She'd never had any complaints from previous lovers about her kissing. Not that she wanted him to kiss her. She wasn't in the market for an affair with the American. Although the thought of a weekend of sex with the muscular man did have its appeal. He'd be gone as soon as the wedding was over, and though she was a world traveler who rarely spent two nights in the same place, she wasn't into that kind of casual relationship.

Kissing the American again would be a mistake.

Then why the hell was she thinking about it to the exclusion of all else? They had a party to arrange for Fiona and Wyatt. The focus should be on them, not on her own carnal needs. Needs she hadn't known she had until he'd kissed her in the airport. The entire time she'd been preparing in her room, she'd gone over and over that kiss. Each time, her body grew warmer and warmer, her heart beating faster as if he was there in the room with her.

Her belly tightened and heat spread at the thought of what it might be like to make love to Mack. Would he be all about vanilla sex? Or would he like a little more action and excitement in bed? A man who spent months in the desert being shot at, always on the edge of being killed, might want stress-free sex. Or was he an adrenaline junkie bent on making sex as dangerous as his life?

"Is this the pub?" Mack asked.

Deirdre came to an abrupt halt and stared at the shingle hanging from the front of the building. Donegal Pub. Damned if it wasn't the pub and she'd almost walked right past. "Yes, this is it." Angry at herself for wool-gatherin', she pushed through the door and charged in.

When the bartender spotted her, he boomed out loud, "Ms. Darcy, I was wonderin' when you'd show yerself."

"Well, I'm here now and I've brought the best man with me. The rest of the crowd will be here shortly."

"I've got the room set up in the back for the womenfolk, seein' as they'd be a might quieter."

"Great. What about music?" she asked, peeling her coat from her shoulders.

"Paddy and Liam O'Connell are comin' to provide traditional Irish ballads, and they also play some of the popular songs."

"Good. Thank you, Mr. Donegal." Deirdre hung her coat on the rack by the door.

"Call me Sean." The rotund bartender held out a hand to Mack. "So yer one of the Magnus brothers?"

Mack gripped the older man's hand. "I am."

"Good to meet you, it 'tis." The big man pulled Mack into a bear hug and pounded his back.

The door behind her opened sending in a draft of cold air and six of Deirdre's cousins.

"Where's the party?" one shouted, clearly already into his cups.

Sean let go of Mack and waved the group in. "If yer here for the weddin' party, yer in the right place. What can I get for ya?"

And so the party began.

Within thirty minutes the pub was full. The other three Magnus brothers arrived. Wyatt had his arm securely looped around a woman's slender waist.

"Fiona, meet my brother, Mack."

The pretty redhead smiled up at him and held out her hand. "Had I known there were four good-looking Magnus brothers, I might have waited to make my choice." She winked as she shook his hand.

"Hey." Wyatt frowned, his arm tightening around her, pulling her flush against his body. "I saw you first."

"I'm just kidding. You know I love you." She leaned up on her toes to kiss Wyatt, the love shining in her eyes. "I just don't want you to get too cocky."

Mack laughed. "You got yourself a feisty one, brother. And a good thing. She'll keep you humble." He pulled Fiona into a quick bear hug. "Welcome to the family."

Fiona and the ladies retired to the room at the rear of the pub where they toasted the bride and gave out advice. Soon music could be heard in the main room of the pub.

"Why are we stayin' back here when there's music on the other side?" Caitlin Mulrooney, Deirdre's cousin from her mother's side, shouted.

The group of women all stood at once, paraded out of the back and crammed into the outer room with the men. A loud roar of approval went up and the dancing began.

Fiona melted into Wyatt's arms and they did a slow dance though the music was a lively Irish jig. When the music slowed to match them, Deirdre couldn't help a sigh. They looked so in love it almost hurt to watch them together.

"Why the big sigh?" a deep voice said close to her ear. "Won't anyone ask you to dance?"

She turned to find Mack standing beside her. "Not so far and they probably won't, considering most of them are my cousins."

"Would you like to dance?"

Knowing it was a mistake, she took his hand and let him lead her to a rare bare spot on the wooden floor. As soon as he pulled her into his arms, she leaned against him and the crowd around them sealed them in the embrace.

"You throw a good party," he said, his words rumbling in his chest. "My brothers have never been to Ireland so this is a treat."

Deirdre tipped her chin up. "Surely your military travels have taken you to foreign countries?"

"Yes, but not where we were truly welcome. It's nice for a change not to have to look where you step or watch behind you for your enemy."

"I can't imagine what it is like to be in a war zone."

"Exhilarating and scary at the same time." He touched a finger beneath her chin. "I'm glad you ladies came out. I was considering going back to my room."

"And miss all this?" She smiled up at him. "It would be a shame to disappoint your brother on the eve of his weddin'."

"He doesn't see anyone else but his bride-to-be."

Deirdre's glance shifted to Wyatt and Fiona, standing in the middle of the floor, barely moving to the beat of the music. "They make a lovely couple."

"They've only known each other for three months. Is that long enough to know whether you're really in love?"

"Some say you know in an instant. Others say their love grew over time." Deirdre envied Wyatt and Fiona. She had always wondered what it would be like to be in love with a man. Her gaze rose to meet Mack's. "Do you believe in love at first sight?"

Mack stared down at her for a long moment.

The fire in his eyes made her blood rush through her veins and her core tighten.

"I don't know about love at first sight. You captured my attention from the moment you first stepped through the door of the terminal."

"I did?"

"Yes. But then I pegged you as an ice queen, dressed in white, hiding behind a scarf and sunglasses, your body ramrod straight."

Deirdre stiffened.

Mack laughed. "Just like that." When she tried to step out of his arms, he tightened them around her. "Then I kissed you and I realized how deceiving looks can be. Beneath the outer shell was a fiery, passionate women." His words ended in a whisper, his head lowering, his mouth sweeping down to claim hers.

As though caught in a time warp, Deirdre couldn't move. Nor did she want to. Since he'd kissed her in the airport, she'd thought of little else. She lifted her face to his and met him, her mouth opening to accept his tongue, her own coming out to sweep across his.

It was as if the world stopped turning and time stood still. Even the music ceased to beat against her ears.

"Hey the song's over, you two." Ronin

bumped against Mack's shoulder. "Come on. I think we're about to start the serious drinking, and I believe you have to get it going with a toast."

Mack broke away from Deirdre, his dark eyes nearly black, his lips wet from hers. He shook his head and focused on the room around him. "Toast? I thought we only did that after the wedding."

"We need more reasons to piss the night away." Sam shoved a mug of beer into Mack's hand and one in Deirdre's as well.

"I didn't think my brothers or any Irishman needed a reason to drink," Mack grumbled. He lifted his mug toward the ceiling. "To my brother, Wyatt and his bride-to-be, Fiona. I wish you all the love your hearts can hold and long, healthy lives together."

The mugs rose in the air to a hearty "Here, here!"

Deirdre raised her mug and drank a long, healthy swallow. She hadn't had a whole mug of beer in the ten years she'd been working as a model. After the first swallow, she tipped the mug and drank it all.

"Hey, slow down there or you'll be crawling under the table before the end of the night." Mack chuckled and took the empty mug from her, setting it on the table.

"That's the first beer I've had since I was a teenager."

"I thought the Irish loved their beer. Why have you waited so long to have another?"

She snorted and wiped her mouth with the back of her hand, feeling a little buzz creeping up on her. "Do you know how many calories there are in one bottle of beer?"

"No, I don't know, but I'm sure you do."

"Sadly, I do—" A hiccup escaped her mouth and she clapped a hand over her lips, her cheeks heating. "Excuse me."

"Here, have another." Sam handed Deirdre another mug full of beer. Before she could think to say no, she was raising it in the air. "To my beautiful cousin Fiona and her fiancé Wyatt, may you both live as long as you want, and never want as long as you live!"

The roar of approval shook the rafters of the old pub.

A slow, sweet melody filled the room. Paddy O'Connell held the microphone and sang with only a guitar as accompaniment. Fiona and Wyatt came together in a tight embrace, swaying to the music.

At the sight of the couple so in love, Deirdre's heart squeezed so tightly that breathing became difficult. She downed half the mug of beer before Mack took it from her hand and set it on the bar.

"Dance with me," he commanded. His voice low, heated and sexy as hell, combined with the effects of the beer, made her completely powerless to resist.

The music and Mack's arms wrapped around her. Deirdre leaned against him, resting her cheek against the side of his neck, the stubble on his chin rasping against her temple. He smelled of soap and male musk, a heady combination, more potent than the alcohol she'd consumed.

A moment later, or so it seemed, the song ended and the O'Connell brothers broke into the Irish song "Finnegan's Wake". The Irish guests all joined in and helped the others who didn't know the words to sing along.

When Deirdre made a move to step out of Mack's embrace, he slipped an arm around her waist and tugged her up against his side.

She didn't argue or try to pull away.

As the noise swelled in the pub, Deirdre longed for the quiet.

"Wanna make a break for it?" Mack asked.

Her heart skipped a couple beats and raced to catch up. "Yes."

Mack clapped his brother Wyatt on the back. "I'm going back to the hotel. Sleep well your last night as a bachelor." He leaned over and kissed Fiona on the cheek. "Are you sure you know what you're getting into?"

She nodded. "I do."

"Did you hear that?" Sam laughed. "She's already practicing to get the words right." He punched Wyatt in the ribs. "You should too."

While his brothers poked fun at Wyatt, Mack gripped Deirdre's hand and he guided her through the crowd to the exit.

She had every chance she needed to tell Mack she wasn't ready to leave, especially with him. The trouble was, she wanted to leave with him. And she didn't want the night to end. Not yet. That first kiss was nothing compared to the one they'd shared during the dance. That one liquefied every bone in her body.

No man had ever inspired such a complete meltdown before. Like a cat was drawn to catnip, she couldn't resist him and followed him willingly, frustrated at the amount of time it took to get through the crush of people in the pub.

At the door, he snagged her jacket from a hook on the wall and held it for her to slide her arms in.

When at last they spilled out into the street, she sucked in a deep breath of chilled, misty air, hoping to cool the heat building inside.

As they started toward the hotel, the mist thickened into rain.

"Come on!" Mack's hand tightened on hers, and they ran to the end of the block and turned. The hotel was only a short distance and they ran hand-in-hand, arriving in the lobby of the hotel, wet and laughing.

Mack didn't stop there, dragging her into the lift, closing the door before anyone else could get in with them. He punched the button for his floor and immediately pulled her into his arms, his mouth crashing down on hers.

What little breath she'd gathered after their mad dash was stolen away in his kiss. It wasn't nearly enough. Before they reached Mack's floor, Deirdre was pushing his jacket from his shoulders and fumbling with the buttons on his shirt.

Tearing her mouth away from his, she pressed a kiss to the side of his throat and to his chest through the gap in his shirt.

The elevator bell rang and the door slid open.

Deirdre grabbed his hand and ran out into the hall. "Which one?"

He pulled his key card from his pocket, kissed her hard on the lips and hurried toward a room near the end of the hall. In seconds he had the door open and they fell through, ripping at each other's clothes.

Mack pushed her jacket off her shoulders, letting it fall to the floor. He unwound the scarf from her neck, tossing it to the side.

Deirdre finished unbuttoning his shirt and shoved it down his arms. She turned, presenting her back and the zipper to her dress to him. "Hurry," she said.

His hands dropped onto her shoulders and he pulled her back against his warm front. "Are you sure?"

She nodded, afraid that if she thought too long, she'd sober up and talk herself out of making love to him.

His fingers moved to the zipper and slid it down her back to the swell of her bottom. "We can stop at the kiss," he said.

"No, we can't." She stepped away from him and turned, sliding the straps of the dress off her shoulders. The garment dropped to the floor at her feet and she stepped out of it. Wearing nothing but black, lace panties and her high heels, she stood in front of him, her chest rising and falling, her breathing ragged.

When he didn't make a move to take her into his arms, she froze, afraid she'd gone too far. Afraid he didn't find her attractive. Afraid of this man's rejection.

Was she insane for throwing herself at him?

Mack locked gazes with Deirdre, refusing to let his eyes feast on her luscious curves. "I thought you didn't want the complications of a quick fling."

"I changed my mind."

He snapped his fingers. "Like that?" Mack shook his head, cursing himself for stalling when she was offering him her body. But the kisses they'd shared had meant more to him than he cared to admit. "If I take you to bed, will you change your mind again?"

"Not tonight," she said.

"After tonight?"

She shook her head. "I'm not here for a relationship. You and I could never work out as a couple. Not in our two careers. I make no guarantees."

"Good. Because I can give no guarantees."

"Then we're good?" She rubbed her naked arms. "Because I'm feeling fairly underdressed here."

"Come here," he commanded.

She complied, sliding into his arms. "Are you not going to get naked as well?" Deirdre glanced up at him, raising her brows.

The sensual invitation in her tone washed over him, making his pulse quicken and his groin tighten. "I was enjoying how soft your skin is and how sexy you look in that outfit."

"Why 'tis nothing but a bit of silk and heels."

"Exactly." His hands slid across her naked back and cupped her bottom, lifting her until her legs wrapped around his waist. Then he turned and pressed her against the wall. He bent to nibble at her earlobe and to brush his lips across the pulse pounding at the base of her throat. "Promise me one thing."

"Saints preserve us. What?" she gasped.

"No regrets."

"The only regret I have is that you are still wearing your clothes." She caught his face between her palms. "Undress already."

"Yes, ma'am." He crushed her lips with his in a swift hard kiss, spun her around and dropped her on the bed.

"Well!" she huffed.

Then with slow deliberation, he shed his shirt and unbuckled his belt.

"Now, you've got it right." She reached out, pushed his hands away from his zipper and slid it down.

His cock sprang free into her palms and heat coiled deep inside of him.

"My, my, you're a big one, are ya?"

"So I've been told," he said through gritted teeth. As long as it had been since he'd had a woman, it wouldn't take much to set him off.

Deirdre ran her hands down his length, cupped his balls and fondled them. "Well, then, let's put this bad boy to use." She slipped out of her panties and flung them to a corner. "Pray tell you know what to do with something this magnificent."

Chapter Three

Mack kicked off his shoes and shucked his trousers. He stood naked in front of Deirdre, enjoying the image she provided. Beautiful with her auburn hair falling down around her pale shoulders, wearing nothing but a pair of bright red stilettos.

She scooted backward across the bed, her lips curling up in a smile. When she was far enough back, she let her legs fall open, exposing her slick, wet entrance to him.

Mack growled low in his throat, every primal instinct since the beginning of time seeming to rise up in him as he crawled up between her legs and leaned over her. "Woman, you make me crazy."

"Still think I'm an ice queen?"

"I'll let you know in the morning." Then he dropped down over her, his chest rubbing against the soft swells of her breasts as he bent to claim her lips. After a long slow twisting of their tongues, he trailed kisses and nips along the smooth line of her jaw and down the slender length of her throat, pausing at the point where her pulse beat beneath the skin. So fast. Her chest rose and fell with every breath, making her nipples brush against him.

One delicious inch at a time, he tasted his way downward, stopping to feast on her breasts, sucking one velvety-soft tip into his mouth, rolling the tip on his tongue until it beaded into a tight little button. While his tongue laved one breast, his hand fondled the other, tweaking and flicking the tip, then moving over her ribs and down her flat belly to that wonderful fluff of hair over her sex.

Her hips rose to greet him as he threaded his fingers between the folds, finding and strumming the narrow strip of flesh between.

Deirdre moaned, her back arching up off the bed. "Jazus! There!"

Mack chuckled, abandoned her breasts and slid his mouth downward over her torso and belly to join his fingers as they played her delicate instrument until she sang out loud.

"Oh Mack, I can't take more." Then, she stiffened, her fingers curling into the comforter. "Yes!" Her body grew rigid and her eyes squeezed shut as she rode the wave of her orgasm to the very end.

He flicked and tongued until she grabbed for his hair and tugged. "I want you. Now. Inside me."

Mack reached over the side of the bed and dug his wallet out of his trousers pocket and fished out one of the little foil packets, thanking his lucky stars he'd had them there from before he'd deployed to Afghanistan.

Deirdre took the packet from him, tore it

open and rolled the condom over his engorged cock. Her warm and gentle fingers guided him to her entrance.

Bracing himself over her, he slid into her wet heat.

Her muscles clenched around him the deeper he went. He eased out, slowly and back in, equally slowly.

Slender fingers closed around his buttocks. "Faster," she said and pulled him toward her.

"I don't want to hurt you."

"I don't care. Give me everything you've got. Hard. Fast. Now!" With her hands, she set the rhythm.

When he matched her pace, her fingers curled around his hips, her nails digging into his skin.

She felt so good. So hot and wet. After over a year without the comfort of a woman's body, Mack was afraid he would shoot the moon too soon. He fought to control himself.

When her long gorgeous legs wrapped around his waist, all bets were off. He drove into her one last time, thrusting as deep as he could go before he stopped and held steady as he catapulted into the stratosphere, his body pulsing with his release.

Minutes later, her legs dropped down beside him and she flung her arms out. "Amazing."

Mack chuckled and he rolled onto his side, taking her with him, still hard inside her. Pulling her close, he liked the way her cheek nestled against his chest. Inhaling deeply, he reveled in her scent.

"Definitely not an ice queen," he pronounced, resting his cheek against her hair.

"I know." Her hand smoothed across his chest, her fingers finding and tweaking his nipples. "It was you who had to be convinced."

He held up a hand like he was swearing in a courtroom. "Color me a believer."

Deirdre pressed her lips against his chest. "A satisfying end to the day."

"More than satisfying." He kissed the top of her hair, his hands gliding down her naked back. "And not the end."

She drew a line down his chest to his navel. "You have more to show me?"

"You bet." His cock stiffened and he surprised himself at how quickly he was ready to go again. He stripped off the condom, grabbed for another and eased it over his cock. Then he rolled onto his back and balanced her on top of him. "Only you get to be on top this time. I'm all for equal opportunity and girl power."

She rose up on her arms and knelt with her knees on either side of him. Then with slow deliberation, she lowered herself over his shaft. "Now this is what I call empowerment," she said, her breath hitching as she rode him. Her breasts bobbed with each rise and fall and her hair bounced around her shoulders.

Mack gripped her hips and slammed her down harder as he impaled her with his thick shaft.

Her channel was so tight around him, her inner muscles clenching, suctioning each time she rose. She was wild and wicked, everything a man could want in bed and more.

Sensations centering in his groin rippled outward, spreading throughout his body like a sunburst, strengthening until they exploded in a fiery torrent. He brought her down hard on him and held her there, his gaze on her face as she flung her hair over her shoulders and arched her back. She clutched her breasts, pinching the nipples as her body shook with the intensity of her orgasm.

For a long moment he held her like that until her shoulders relaxed and his own body unwound.

Deirdre lay across his chest, her cheek resting on his neck. "I could fall asleep like this," she said, her voice barely above a whisper.

"Then why don't you?"

She shook her head. "I need to go."

Mack stiffened, his cock twitching inside her in protest. "Go? Why?"

"If I stay and the paparazzi get wind of it, you'll never have a moment's rest. They'll want to know all the dirty little details of our relationship." She rolled off him and stood beside the bed, still wearing her stilettos and nothing else, her hands on her hips. "And since we agreed we aren't in a relationship and don't have the time or the physical proximity to conduct one, I don't want to bother answering questions about you, any more than have already been asked."

Mack sat up, frowning. "So that's it?"

She smiled. "Other than the wedding

tomorrow, I probably won't be seeing you again. You'll be on your way to wherever you go with the military, and I'll be on to my next modeling engagement."

He didn't like how matter-of-fact she was and couldn't fathom how she could jump right up and rush out of the room after such a soul-shattering orgasm. "I'll be here a couple days."

"Really? You should take a tour of Dublin while you're here." She gathered her clothes.

Mack swung his legs over the side of the bed, peeled the condom off and slung it into the trash. Then he stood, capturing her hips in his hands as she bent to collect her panties. He pulled her bottom against his still stiff member. "Stay."

"I can't." She straightened, her back rigid against his chest.

"You can." Sliding his hands upward, he cupped her breasts in his palms and massaged them until the nipples budded. "Show me Dublin from a native's perspective."

"I haven't lived in Dublin for years. You're better off catching one of the tour buses," she insisted.

"I don't want a tour. I want you." Mack pushed aside her hair and nibbled at the back of her neck.

A moan rose from her throat and she melted against him.

While one hand continued to fondle her breast, he slid the other down her front to the juncture of her thighs, cupping her sex, his pulse hammering. "Stay the night." He couldn't let her go. Not now. The image of her walking toward him in the airport, wearing the cold white jacket, flashed in his mind. He'd thought her icy, possibly frigid. She'd proved to be a deliciously warm contrast. And now that he knew what fire lay beneath the disguise, beneath her skin and in her heart, he couldn't let it end so soon. He'd just gotten a taste for Deirdre and it left him craving more.

She dropped her clothes at her feet and slid her arms behind her to cup his buttocks, pressing him to her, his cock nudging her behind.

He backed a step and another until his legs bumped against the bed as he parted her folds and stroked that nubbin of flesh that made her purr like a kitten.

Deirdre moaned again, her legs easing apart, her bottom rubbing against him.

Mack flicked and coaxed her clit while he pinched her nipple between the thumb and forefinger of his other hand.

She writhed, her body undulating like the ebb and flow of waves. "Too much," she whispered.

He spun with her in his arms and turned her to face him as he lifted her to sit on the edge of the bed. Then he nudged her knees apart and dropped down between them and started laying kisses along the insides of her thighs, first the right one, then the left. Starting at the curve of her knee, he worked his way closer to her damp entrance, glistening with the dew of her excitement.

With his fingers, he parted her folds, pressing a thumb into her channel. "Stay," he whispered, blowing a warm stream of air over her pussy. His gaze locked with hers as he flicked his tongue out, tapping her clit.

Her chest rose on a swiftly indrawn breath, her eyes widening as he flicked her again. "You're making it hard to say no."

"Then say yes." He flicked her again then swiped his tongue in a long, steady caress along the narrow strip of densely packed nerve endings, praying he hit the right spot.

She let go of the breath she'd been holding and said, "Okay, you win. But only a little while longer." Deirdre dug her fingers into his scalp and held him close, while he sucked, nibbled, tongued and nipped her clit.

He wanted more, but any time she was willing to give him was better than none. He vowed to make her want to stay with every flick of his finger, stroke of his tongue and caress.

Hours later, Deirdre lay spooned against Mack's body, his arm draped over her hip. She'd had more orgasms in one night than with any of her other lovers. Perhaps she'd been too busy to experiment with her other partners. Who was she kidding? Her lovers had only been concerned about their own satisfaction.

Not Mack. He'd taken his time ensuring she had the orgasms to beat all orgasms. He'd tweaked, teased and coaxed not one but multiple incredible releases. At one point, she thought she heard herself scream.

Mack had been gentle at first, then increasingly demanding until she had abandoned all resistance and gone along with the big marine. Now, she lay in the dark, feeling like she'd come home, like there was no other place she'd rather be. And it scared the hell out of her.

She had her career and Mack had his. The stress of traveling to new locations every week or every other week had taken their toll on her. Just last week, she'd been thumbing through pictures of cottages in quiet towns, mountain retreats, desert islands, thinking about taking a vacation, something she hadn't done in a very long time. Perhaps that was all she needed. Slow down. Take some time off. Sleep in.

But not with a man she could get used to having around much too easily. No. Mack Magnus was far too tempting. Deirdre could see her wanting more and more time with him. The few men she'd slept with left her feeling empty. One night in the sack and she was done, never wanted to see them again.

That's what had her scared about Mack. Sex with Mack left her wanting more. Even as she lay there, curled into him, her body heated. If she turned over and kissed him, it could only lead to one thing.

More of Mack.

Like an addiction, she fought her cravings and

slid out from beneath his arm and off the bed. Deirdre gathered her clothing and dressed as quickly as possible, careful not to make a sound to disturb the sleeping giant. If he woke, he'd talk her into staying again and she'd find it impossible to resist.

No use getting her knickers in a twist over a man who wouldn't be around for longer than the wedding weekend. And she was due to fly out on Monday to the Caribbean island of Tortuga to shoot a swimsuit ad for a magazine. Mack would go one way, she'd go another and they'd likely never see each other again.

Grabbing her purse, she clutched her shoes by the straps and draped her coat and scarf over her arm. Then she eased open the door to the room, glanced at Mack lying peacefully asleep and almost changed her mind. Before she could, she backed out of the room and closed the door softly behind her.

She swung around and slammed into a large, burly man in a black suit with a mobile phone pressed to his ear, his knuckles black with crisscrossing tattoos, like those she'd seen on some of the Travelers in the lobby earlier that evening. The man dropped his phone and staggered backward with the force of the impact.

Deirdre dropped everything in her hands to keep from falling flat on her face. The contents of her purse spilled out on the ground, her cell phone sliding across the floor.

"Shite!" she muttered, bending to collect her

things, shoving lipstick, mints, a comb and her phone into her purse. "Pardon me, sir."

The big man glared at her, bent to snatch his mobile phone from the ground and pushed past her, nearly knocking her off her feet again. Another man exited the room beside Mack's and closed the door, his eyes widening when he saw Deirdre standing there.

Smaller than the first man, but equally as intimating, this one had a scar on his cheek from the corner of his eye to the corner of his lip. Even without the jagged scar, he made Deirdre shake. He slipped his hand into his jacket pocket, his dark brows forming a V over the bridge of his nose.

Embarrassed at her clumsiness and frightened by his attitude, she slipped her purse over her shoulder, grabbed her jacket and shoes and straightened, moving out of the way so the man could ease by. She hadn't blocked the hallway so what the feck was the matter with him and the first jerk? When you practically bowl a lady over you apologize, whether it was your fault or not.

For a moment, the man hesitated, his eyes black and narrowed. Something tented in the jacket pocket he'd slid his hand in, reminding Deirdre of the old movies with cops and robbers when the bad guy held a hidden gun. The ferocity of the man's stare sent a cold shiver across Deirdre's arms and she took an involuntary step backward, bumping into the wall. For a moment she was frozen, caught in the intensity of the man's stare.

The dark-eyed menace edged forward and said something in a language she didn't understand.

The big man's glance shifted from the little guy to her, and he took a step toward her, his arms rising, reaching for her.

Backing away, Deirdre's breath caught and held. *Shite! Shite! Shite!* She had nowhere to run. The door to Mack's room had locked behind her and she was trapped between the two men.

"Deirdre?" Mack's voice called out from the other side of the hotel room door.

The big man glanced toward the sound and back to her. Then he ducked his head and hurried past her, the shorter man following close behind as the door to Mack's room jerked open.

Mack stood in his jeans, the zipper half done up, the top button hanging open. "Deirdre?" He stepped out into the hallway and pulled her into his arms. "What's wrong?"

"Nothing, now that you're here," she said, melting into his embrace. A shiver shook her body and she snuggled closer. "Let's go back inside." As he led her into his room, Deirdre glanced over her shoulder.

The scar-faced man who'd stared at her with such menace had disappeared.

Once inside the room with the door firmly shut, Deirdre sagged against Mack, wrapping her arms around his waist.

He hugged her close. "Why did you leave?"

Funny how silly her fear of falling for Mack

compared to the fear she'd experienced in the hallway with the two dark-haired men who'd come out of the room beside Mack's. She laughed, shakily. "I was scared."

"Of me?" He rubbed her back, the soothing circles of his hand calming her.

"No, of myself. I was afraid that the more I was with you, the more I'd get used to having your around."

"I know what you mean." He leaned his cheek against her temple. "We're worlds apart in our careers and countries." Mack leaned away from her, tipping her chin up with his finger. "But that doesn't explain the fear in your eyes when I opened the door. You're still shaking."

"I ran into two men in the hallway."

Mack stiffened. "Did they hurt you?"

"No. I bumped into one. Other than dropping everything, it didn't hurt."

"Did they say anything to you that frightened you?"

"No." Deirdre shook her head. "It was more a feeling."

"Well, next time you feel scared, you can tell me. And for whatever reason you want to leave, I'll walk you to your room." He kissed her forehead. "If you'd like me to walk you to your room right now, I will."

Deirdre leaned up on her toes and kissed his lips. "No. I want to stay here."

"You're not scared of me or what's happening between us?"

"Not as scared as I was with the men the hallway."

Mack laughed. "Thanks, I think."

She took his hand. "Could we go back to bed?"

He grinned. "You have to ask?" He lifted her fingers to his lips and pressed a kiss to the backs of her knuckles. "Come on. I don't know about you, but I need sleep." He led her to the bed, took her jacket from her and draped it over the back of a nearby chair.

She lifted her arms and he dragged her dress up over her head, laying it neatly over the jacket.

Deirdre shimmied out of her panties and slid onto the bed.

Mack's eyes flared as she lay across the sheets.

Slowly, he shed his jeans and stood beside the bed, naked. "Sleep. That's all we're going to do, right? I've been up for thirty-six hours. I don't think I have anything left in me."

Deirdre jerked her head to the side. "Get in the feckin' bed. I promise not to attack you."

"Good." He grinned as he lay on the mattress beside her. "I'm really tired." His hand smoothed across her naked skin, his cock rising despite his protestations to the opposite.

"Nothing left in ya, is it?" She stroked the length of him and he grew even thicker and longer. "Got any more of those condoms secreted away in your wallet?"

"If not, I bet I have one in my shaving kit."

"Are you one of those American boy scouts

and always prepared?"

He held up two fingers. "Yes, ma'am."

Deirdre didn't let Mack go back to sleep until the first light of dawn crept in through the window. He had a lot more in him than he let on, and she was determined to banish all the bad feelings she'd gotten from her unexpected encounter in the hallway.

She finally fell asleep, wrapped in Mack's arms, exhausted and more content than she cared to admit.

As soon as her eyes closed, the dream began with a woman's scream. Whether it was her own scream or another woman's wasn't important. Two men raced out of a hotel room, running straight for her. She tried to get out of the way, but they were coming too fast. When she moved her feet, it was as if they were glued to the floor. She fought to lift them, but she couldn't.

"Help!" she cried.

Chapter Four

Mack had been in a dead sleep when he heard Deirdre's cry. He sat up straight, ready to take on the enemy only to find the enemy was in Deirdre's dreams.

He leaned over her, shaking her shoulder, pressing kisses to her cheek. "Deirdre, wake up."

"Help," she sobbed, her fingers curling into his arms, digging in.

Ignoring the pain, Mack shook her again. "Deirdre, wake up. You're having a bad dream."

Her eyes flew open, wide and frightened. When she finally recognized him, she wrapped her arms around him and buried her face in his chest.

"It's okay," he whispered, rubbing her back. The feel of her breasts pressed against his chest was more than he could take. His cock hardened instantly, but he fought his natural reaction to her beautiful body. She didn't need him pawing on her when she was clearly upset. "It was just a dream."

"I know," she said. "But it seemed so real."

"It's morning. The sun is up and you're safe with me."

"Thank you." She stared up at him, her dark

red hair falling over her cheek, shadowing her eyes.

He brushed the strands out of her face. "Are you okay?"

"I am now." She smiled. "That dream seemed so real and no matter hard I tried, I couldn't run."

"I've had dreams like that. Part of them are memories of skirmishes I was involved in. Sometimes they're worse than what really happened. Other times, they're dead on. Memories I'd just as soon forget." He pressed his lips together, images of some of the worst battles rearing in his mind. Times he'd rather forget but were engraved into thoughts. Times when they'd been hit by enemy fire and he'd held one of his men in his arms as he bled out. The medic could do nothing to save him.

Deirdre's slim fingers curled around his cheek. "Your memories are far more frightening than mine. How can you live with them?"

He shrugged. "I take each day one at a time. Some days are harder than others, but I figure I'm here for a reason. I'd better make good on that reason." He kissed the tip of her nose. "What were you dreaming about?"

"The men in the hallway last night."

"They're gone now, and you're safe with me."

Deirdre pressed her lips to his chest. "Thank you for letting me sleep here last night."

Mack laughed, shaking off the morose memories of days in battle. "You're kidding, right? I should be thanking you." His hand slid over her hip and upward to rest on the curve of her narrow waist. "For letting me hold such a beautiful, naked woman all night long." God, he wanted her so badly it hurt. But if she wanted to make love, she'd have to come to him. He wouldn't initiate it this time.

Deirdre trailed her fingers down his chest and lower to where his cock jutted out hard and full. "Are you always so amorous in the morning?" she asked.

"Not so much around a unit full of men." As her hand wrapped around him, Mack sucked in a deep breath and held it.

She glanced up, a wicked gleam in her blue eyes. "Then what are you waiting for?"

"You to tell me you want more than a kiss good morning," he said through gritted teeth.

"I want a lot more than a kiss good morning." She moved her hand up and down his cock, the friction jerking him wide awake, all thoughts of sleep completely vanquished.

"In that case..." he rolled her onto her back and leaned over her, nudging her legs apart with his knee, "...good morning." He captured her lips in a crushing kiss.

When he came up for air, she smiled. "That's more like it."

He stared into her eyes, barely able to believe his luck at having found her, but not willing to mess things up. "Don't move." He leaped from the bed and hurried for the bathroom where he kept his shaving kit. When he returned to the room with an accordion of condoms in his hand, she was lying on her side, touching her breasts.

His breath caught and he nearly stumbled. "You're beautiful."

She winked. "So I've been told."

Mack laughed. "Modest much?"

"It comes from being a model. I can take it or leave it."

"How about this?" He slid into the bed with her. "You're beautiful where it counts." He tapped a finger to her chest. "Inside."

"Now, you're getting warmer." She took his hand and laid it across her breast.

He cupped it, weighing it in his palm. "Perfect. Exactly the right size for a man to hold and taste."

"Show me."

He laughed, feeling lighter and more carefree than he had in a very long time. "Aren't you afraid we'll be late for the wedding?"

"The wedding isn't until noon and we have an hour before I have to be at the beauty shop with Fiona."

"Isn't that cutting it close?"

"Only if you keep talking and don't get busy."

"Yes, ma'am." He leaned over to snatch her scarf from the floor. "Let's get things straight. I like giving the orders, and I might just keep you captive the whole day and skip the wedding altogether." He wrapped the silk scarf around one of her wrists. "Are you game?"

She bit her bottom lip, her eyes shining. "I'll play along until I have to go."

"Until I let you leave." He captured her other wrist and wound the scarf loosely around it and tied it to the bedpost, securing her wrists.

Deirdre pouted. "How am I supposed to touch you?"

"You don't. I get to do with you as I please."

Her brows furrowed. "I'm not sure I trust you."

"Honey, when I'm finished, you won't care." He started at her forehead, kissing his way over her nose and to her mouth, where he spent time teasing her lips until she opened to him. He caressed her tongue with his in long, slow strokes.

Then he moved lower, kissing a path along the line of her jaw, down the column of her throat to where the pulse beat hard beneath her skin.

"Let me touch you," she moaned, pulling against her bindings. "Please."

"In time," he assured her, his hands cupping her breasts to plump them for his tasting. He flicked the tip of one, the nipple tightening into a hardened bead. He licked it then sucked it into his mouth.

Deirdre arched her back, pressing the breast deeper. "Lower."

"Lower please?" he insisted.

"Jazus, Mary and Joseph. Lower, pleeeease," she moaned.

Mack chuckled. "As you wish." He released her breasts, his hands moving low over her flat belly, dipping into her belly button and downward to the juncture of her thighs.

Her breathing grew more ragged the lower he went.

Trailing kisses along the path his hands took, he paused at the mound of red curls. "Are you ready? Or do you need more convincing?"

She lifted her head, her eyes glazed with passion. "Ready! I'm ready. Oh please, ride me for feck's sake," she begged. Bringing her knees up, she dug her heels into the bed and lifted her hips, urging him closer.

When his fingers threaded through her curls to part her folds, she dropped her knees to the side, exposing her entrance, glistening with her juices.

Mack fought his growing desire, holding back to completely pleasure her before taking what he so desperately wanted. He wanted her so ready she'd shout his name.

He touched her clit, dragging his finger along its short length.

Deirdre bucked, her body twisting in the sheets. "Again. Please," she cried.

Sliding his body down hers, he settled between her knees, lifting her legs to drape over his shoulders. Then he cupped her bottom and spread her folds with his thumbs. "Prepare to come undone," he whispered, blowing a soft stream of air over her wet center.

"I already am," she cried.

"You only think you are" Already so hard he hurt, Mack's cock twitched, ready to thrust deep inside her. He held out. This was Deirdre's moment.

He touched his tongue to her entrance, tasting her musk, then he replaced his tongue with a finger, pushing it in as he swept upward to tongue the nerve-packed nubbin of her desire.

"Sweet Jazus!" Deirdre cried.

Mack tongued her again then laved her in long broad strokes.

Her hips rocked with each stroke until her body grew rigid and she stopped all movement. "Oh, sweet mother, if I die now, so be it," she whispered. Then the first waves of her release rippled across her body.

Mack didn't let up, still tonguing her until she tossed her head back and forth. "Stop, oh, stop. I can't take more. It's too much."

Unable to wait another moment, Mack slipped Deirdre's legs off his shoulders and grabbed for a little foil packet. He tore it open and rolled the condom over his engorged, throbbing dick, and then he drove into Deirdre.

She dug her heels into the mattress, meeting him thrust for thrust.

Already so tense with passion, it wasn't long before Mack burst over the edge and came, the moment so earth-shattering he could barely breathe. For several minutes, he remained buried inside her. Finally, he reached for the silk scarf and untied her wrists, then he collapsed on the bed, rolling her to her side to maintain their intimate connection.

Deirdre breathed like a runner who'd been

sprinting. When she could talk again, she said, "Well done."

Mack burst out laughing, pulling her into his arms to hold her tight. He could get used to holding Deirdre. She fit him perfectly.

Deirdre hugged him, reveling in how good it felt to be held in such a strong man's embrace. She could get used to being with this big American marine.

"Nightmare gone?" he asked, his breath warm against her hair.

"What nightmare?" she said. It was true. The nightmare had long faded with Mack's determined assault on her senses.

Then he smacked her bare bottom with the palm of his hand, the sound greater than the actual sting. The little bit of pain sending shards of desire through her. "You need to get going. My brother's bride needs her cousin's assistance to prepare for a wedding."

She moaned and snuggled closer. "I'd rather stay here."

His arms tightened around her. "I'd rather we both stayed here."

Deirdre sighed and leaned back. "Alas, duty calls." She kissed his lips and rolled out of the bed before she gave in to her desire to stay in bed all day with Mack.

Mack leaned up on an elbow, his long, lean and magnificently muscled body on full display. "Save a dance for me."

"Okay," she said. And why not? A few short hours ago, she'd been running out of the room, determined to put distance between him and her. Now she couldn't wait to see him again and she hadn't even left his presence. What was wrong with her? She didn't have time in her life for a relationship. But then this wasn't a relationship. This was a weekend fling.

She gathered her clothes for the third time, regret tugging at her.

Turning her back to get him out of her sight, she lifted her wrinkled dress over her head.

Large hands cupped her breasts from behind. "Sorry, I couldn't resist copping one last feel." He squeezed her breasts and then slid his hands down her torso to the triangle of hair over her mons. Mack stroked her clit and dipped a finger into her damp channel still wet from making love with him.

Caught with her dress raised over her head, she could do nothing to stop him. Nor did she want to.

As quickly as he started, he stepped back, grabbed the hem of the dress and pulled it down over her head and shoulders, his knuckles skimming her skin, sending delightful tingles all over her body. Her pussy clenched. When the dress covered her hips, she turned in his arms. "You're making it very difficult for me to leave."

"That was the idea."

"But I have to go."

"I know. And now, hopefully, you'll want to come back."

"I'm making no promises." She tapped the tip of her finger to his lips. "You're a dangerous addiction I might not be able to overcome."

"Good." He kissed her finger, brushed it aside and kissed her on the lips. "Go before I take you back to bed."

After slipping into her shoes, she straightened. "I'll see you on the other side of the groom." She winked and turned away to grip the doorknob.

When she hesitated, Mack pushed her hand aside. "Let me check the hallway first."

"You can't open the door naked."

He grinned. "Sure I can. Watch." He yanked open the door. A large woman in a short dress that barely covered her ass or her breasts was passing by in the hallway. She stopped in front of the door. Her gaze swept his length and then shifted to Deirdre. "When you're done with him, I'll take some of that." Her finger pointed to his cock. With a wink, she walked away.

Deirdre giggled. "Served you right."

Mack stared after the woman. "I don't know. She was kind of hot with all that makeup."

Even though Mack's voice and glance was teasing, Deirdre couldn't help the little stab of jealousy that shot through her. She backhanded him in his bare abdomen as she slid past him and out into the hallway. "She can have you on Monday."

He snagged her arm and pulled her up against his naked chest. "Does that mean you're mine for the weekend?"

A thrill of anticipation made her shiver. She forced herself to shrug. "Maybe."

He tipped her chin with his finger. "Maybe, hell. You'll be back." He kissed her, turned her around and slapped her ass. "Now, go. Or the bride will be frantic."

Deirdre hurried down the hallway toward the lift, glancing back as she stepped in. Mack still stood in the doorway, as naked as the day he was born. The door to the lift almost closed before she pulled herself together enough to bring her face inside. Even after the doors closed, the naked marine's image was seared into her mind. She fanned herself as the car headed up to her floor.

She hurried to her room, took a quick shower, dressed in tailored trousers, a wool blazer and comfortable shoes. Then she slipped her jacket on and headed for Fiona's room.

She knocked once and the door was flung open.

Fiona stood there, her hair wet and tangled, wearing a camisole and panties and nothing else. "Thank God you're here." She grabbed Deirdre's arm and yanked her into the room. "I've been trying to get hold of you for the past hour. First, I got a strange man, then nothing. Did you turn off your cell phone?"

"No, I didn't hear it ring." She set her purse, scarf and jacket on a chair and gripped Fiona's arms. "I'm here now. What's wrong?"

"Nothing. Oh, everything!" Fiona flung her hands in the air and spun away. She paced to the head of the bed and back. "It's my wedding day and I can't think straight. What am I supposed to wear? Where am I supposed to go first? I'm an event planner, for heaven's sake. I should know all of this!"

Deirdre laughed. "You're going to be just fine. Let good ol' Deirdre help." She walked to the closet and selected a pair of jeans and a white button-up blouse. "Put these on. You don't have to be gorgeous until you're wearing your wedding dress. First stop is the hairdresser's."

Fiona hugged Deirdre as she held the clothes. "Thank you for being here for me."

A twinge of guilt pulled at Deirdre. She'd been ready to tell Fiona to fend for herself as she gave in to her own lusty desire to stay in bed with Mack. She hugged her cousin and pushed the clothes into her arms. "Get dressed. We have to be at the shop in ten minutes."

"Ten minutes!" Fiona flung her arms in the air again and the clothes flew to the sides. "Holy hell." She bent to gather them. "I've never been so nervous in my life."

"You know you can change your mind about marrying Wyatt all the way up to the altar."

With her jeans halfway up her legs, she stopped and stared at Deirdre. "Change my mind? Are you crazy? Wyatt's everything I could have ever dreamed of in a husband."

"Then why are you so nervous?"

"If I don't get to him first, some other woman might snatch him up." She flung her hands in the air again and almost tripped over her jeans. "Until I get a ring on his finger, he's still up for grabs. Have you seen him? He's gorgeous!"

Deirdre laughed and steadied her cousin. "Oh Fiona, you have nothing to worry about." At the same time she said it, she envisioned Mack. All the Magnus brothers were well-built and so ruggedly handsome a woman would have to be blind not to appreciate them. Especially Mack. She shook herself out of her musings to add, "I've seen the way Wyatt looks at you. He loves you."

Fiona's eyes welled with unshed tears. "You think so? Really?"

Deirdre held Fiona's hands and nodded. "Absolutely. The man is head over heels." Even as she said the words, she wondered how it would feel to have Mack look at her that way. She squeezed Fiona's fingers and nodded toward her jeans. "Now hurry. You want to look your best. This is supposed to be the most important day of your life."

"You're right." She yanked her jeans up over her hips and jammed her arms into the white blouse. "I'm getting married." Her eyes welled.

"Oh for Pete's sake, don't cry, you'll make your eyes red and puffy." Deirdre grabbed a tissue from a box in the bathroom and shoved it into Fiona's hands. While her cousin dabbed at her eyes, Deirdre buttoned her shirt. "Now slip on your shoes and jacket and let's go."

They were ten minutes late to the hair and makeup appointment, but the stylists were ready and waiting. They should have been, Deirdre knew them personally and had paid them plenty to be there. When they were through at the stylists' shop, Deirdre had a hired car waiting to collect them out front and ferry them to the church a good hour and a half before the wedding was due to begin.

A pretty, black-haired young woman waited in the antechamber that had been designated for the bride and her bridesmaids to dress for the wedding.

The young woman planted her fists on her hips. "I'm so glad you two finally arrived. I thought I was going to have to inform the guests there was to be no wedding. Then I was going to go hunting for the woman who broke my brother's heart. And I'm a damned good shot." She stuck out her hand. "Hello, I'm Abby Magnus, I presume one of you is Fiona?"

Fiona's eyes softened and she gripped the woman's hand. "You're Abby?" She pulled the woman into a big hug. "You look like your brothers."

"God, I hope not." Abby laughed, light dancing in her eyes.

"You're much smaller, but you have the same black hair and blue eyes."

"We got that from our mother. She was beautiful." Abby stepped back. "I brought my dress and it won't take long to get into it. What do you need help with?"

The women went about dressing the bride in

her form-fitting white gown that hugged her body to perfection. Abby adorned her neck with a single strand of pearls, while Deirdre helped her slip the pale green garter up her leg.

Abby and Deirdre dressed in simple, sage-green gowns and matching ballet slippers.

With only a few minutes to spare before the ceremony, Abby hurried around the room, lifting plastic bags, clothes and purses. Finally she straightened, a worried frown on her face. "Fiona, where's your veil?"

Fiona smiled. "I chose not to wear a veil." She reached into a box and pulled out a delicate wreath of miniature pale pink rosebuds and the soft green bells of Ireland threaded through the band. When she positioned it on her long auburn curls, the effect was magical, making her appear as light and whimsical as a mystical fairy.

Deirdre's eyes washed with tears. "Fiona, you're lovely." Then she hugged her cousin so tightly Fiona protested.

"Careful, sweetie, I'll need my breath to make it down the aisle." Fiona turned to the mirror for the first time since she'd come into the antechamber. Her eyes widened and a gasp left her lips. "Wow, is that me?"

"Yes, indeed, it 'tis," Deirdre said stepping up behind her.

Abby claimed the other side and smiled into the mirror. "You make a beautiful bride. As long as you don't break my brother's heart, I couldn't be happier for you two."

Deirdre laughed. "Are all Magnus siblings this protective of each other?"

"Damn right," Abby answered, crossing her arms. The petite young woman looked no less intimidating for her short stature.

Fiona raised her hand. "I swear I won't break Wyatt's heart. He's my hero. I can't imagine being with any other man."

"Good, then let's go to a wedding." Abby held out her arm.

Fiona hooked her arm with the younger Magnus sibling and one with Deirdre. "Ladies, get me to the church on time."

"Uh, Fiona darlin', you're in the church," Deirdre said, her expression deadpan.

The three women laughed out loud.

A light knock on the door and a head poked through.

Deirdre's heart skipped several beats when she recognized Mack.

"Everyone ready?"

"We're ready," Abby replied.

His gaze captured Deirdre's and he winked, setting her heart to racing. "See you in a few."

Deirdre touched a hand to her chest, reminding herself to breathe. The man shouldn't have that big of an effect on her.

When she dragged her gaze away from the door Mack had disappeared through, she caught Fiona and Abby staring at her.

"Wanna tell me what's going on between you and my brother Mack?" Abby asked.

Heat rose in Deirdre's cheeks. "Nothing."

"Sure you don't have anything to tell us?" Fiona asked.

"Nope. Nothing." That was Deirdre's story and she was sticking to it.

Abby left the room first to clear the way for Fiona.

Deirdre tidied their things, tucking her purse beneath her jacket. At that exact moment, her cell phone rang.

Her pulse leaped. Could it be Mack calling her to tell her he couldn't wait to see her at the end of the aisle? She yanked her purse out from beneath her jacket and rifled through it until her hand curled around her phone. She hit the key to talk. "Hello," she said, her voice breathy.

For a long moment the caller held the line but didn't say anything. If not for the sound of heavy breathing, Deirdre would have thought it was a dropped call.

"Who is this?" she asked.

No one answered. Something clicked and the call ended.

Disappointed, she shoved the phone back into her purse and hid it beneath her coat. Then she ran to catch up to bride.

Chapter Five

Abby led the way down the aisle first. Followed by Deirdre and Fiona.

At the end of the rows of pews stood all four of the Magnus brothers, each of them dark-haired, blue-eyed and handsome as the devil himself.

Deirdre's heart fluttered and a storm of butterflies battered their wings inside her belly. She felt as though she was the one marching down the aisle to meet her true love to exchange vows. Her footsteps faltered. Then her gaze sought out Mack's and locked with his.

Her feet grew more sure, and soon she was mounting the steps to the dais, standing on the opposite side of the groom from Mack.

While all others stared at Fiona coming down the aisle, Mack's gaze remained on Deirdre's until Fiona stepped up beside Wyatt and passed Deirdre her bouquet.

The trance broken, Deirdre reminded herself whose marriage they were there to attend. She should not be having fanciful wedding ideas about Mack. It could never be. They'd only just met one another. One day and one night in bed did not make a binding relationship.

Deirdre tried to focus on the priest and the words he spoke, but all too soon, her gaze was drawn back to Mack like a bee to honey. And, damn the man, he was looking across at her.

Determined to keep her mind on the wedding at hand, Deirdre turned in time to note the priest had come to the vows.

Wyatt took Fiona's hands in his and they both spoke loud and clearly enough for all to hear.

"We swear by love and peace to stand,
Heart to heart and hand in hand.
O Spirit, hear us now,
Confirming this, our sacred vow."

Fiona turned to Deirdre.

Deirdre handed her the simple platinum wedding band engraved with their wedding date on the inside.

Fiona slipped the band on Wyatt's left ring finger. "With this ring, I promise to love you and honor you above all others. I promise to be patient and forgiving and to always have a sense of humor. And you know how hard that can be for me." Her voice caught on a sob, but she continued, "Most of all, I promise to be a true and loyal friend to you always. My heart is yours."

Wyatt turned to Mack who handed him a smaller wedding band. He took the ring and slid it onto Fiona's finger. "I can't promise that I will always be at your side, but I can promise that you will always be in my heart. No matter where I go, I promise that my love and commitment to you will remain strong. I will respect, encourage and cherish you for all the days of my life. I love you."

The priest pronounced them husband and wife.

Wyatt swept Fiona up in his arms and kissed her long and passionately. When the couple came up for air, the love shining from their eyes could not be denied. A cheer rose into the rafters and tears trickled down Deirdre's cheeks.

She handed Fiona her bouquet of white lilies and the couple swept down the aisle to the exit.

Deirdre laid her hand on Mack's arm and followed Fiona and Wyatt down the aisle. She and Abby broke off to gather everything from the antechamber then hurried out of the church. Cars were lined up ready to whisk them off to the hotel where the reception was to take place in the same ballroom the Travelers' wedding had taken place in the night before.

The room had been transformed into an elegant display of cloth-covered tables with candles glowing as centerpieces. A long table on a raised dais was where the couple would be sitting. Deirdre ditched their clothing and purses behind that table and joined the crowd gathered around the happy couple.

Wyatt stood beside Fiona at the entrance, smiling down at her as one after another guests arrived and congratulated them. As the guests arrived, champagne was handed around by hotel staff members.

When everyone had a glass, Mack stepped

forward. "A toast to my brother and his new wife. May all your joys be pure joy and all your pain be champagne. I love you, brother, and wish you all the happiness you both deserve."

Deirdre lifted her glass with the crowd and shouted, "Here! Here!"

More toasts were offered and finally the band in the corner struck up a waltz. Fiona and Wyatt stepped onto the dance floor and performed their first dance as a married couple. Then Wyatt's father asked to dance with Fiona, while his mother danced with Wyatt.

Once their dances were over, Mack headed across the floor, making a beeline for Deirdre.

Her heart thundered against her ribs and she nearly passed out before she realized she was holding her breath.

When Mack was only three steps away from her, one of the hotel managers intervened, catching his arm.

Mack continued to stare across at Deirdre until the man said something that made him transfer his gaze to the staff member. His brows angled together into a deep glaring V. "What?" he said, loud enough Deirdre could hear him. He shot another glance in Deirdre's direction and then spun on his heels and followed the staff member from the ballroom.

Deirdre hurried after them. In the lobby, several uniformed members of the Garda were huddled with the hotel manager and staff.

"When did it happen?" Mack was asking.

The Garda officer he was speaking to responded, "The coroner estimates some time in the middle of the night."

Deirdre stepped up to the officer. "What's going on?"

The hotel manager shot a look around and then spoke quietly. "There's been a murder."

Mack hooked Deirdre's arm as her knees buckled.

"A murder?" She shook her head. "What does that have to do with Mack?"

The officer in charge turned to her. "It occurred in the room adjacent to his. We brought him out of the celebration to ask if he'd heard or seen anything last night that would indicate who might have killed the occupant of the room."

Another Garda member's face lit up. "You're Deirdre Darcy, aren't you?"

Deirdre nodded.

The man stepped forward. "Wait 'til I tell me wife. She'll be right jealous when she gets wind of me meetin' you and all."

Mack lifted a hand to keep the man from getting too close.

It didn't faze the man. "My wife collects all yer magazine ads. I loved ya in the makeup commercial. That bikini was—"

His boss stepped in. "Save it for the pub, Cavan. We have an investigation to conduct."

Deirdre leaned against Mack.

Mack slid an arm around Deirdre's waist and

held her up as she seemed about to fall. He didn't like how pale she'd become.

"Sir, can you tell me where you were between midnight and four o'clock in the morning?"

"I was in my room." Mack frowned. "Why?"

"You were the closest to the deceased. We have to ask."

"Is he being accused of the murder?" Deirdre demanded.

"No, but being as close as he was, he's a person of interest."

Her back stiffened and she stepped forward. "I can verify he was in his room for the entire time."

"How could you, unless you were with—" The detective's face flushed scarlet.

"Were ya with Miss Darcy?" the detective named Cavan asked, his eyes widening. "I'd give me left nut to be with her. No offense to me wife. I wouldn't cheat on her for just any woman."

"Shut up, Cavan. Better yet, go sit in the vehicle."

"But—" Cavan glanced from Deirdre to Mack and back to Deirdre. "I really do have the utmost respect for you, Miss Darcy."

"Go." The detective pointed to the exit.

Cavan's shoulders drooped as he slumped toward the exit. "Wait'll the boys at O'Brien's hear about this."

As Cavan was leaving the hotel, a female television reporter slipped in with her cameraman.

"Here we go." Deirdre turned her face into

Mack's shirt.

"Excuse me, I'm Siobhan Callahan from Channel 4 News. I understand there's been a murder here at the hotel. Can you tell me more?" She held her microphone like a weapon, brandishing it in the face of the detective.

"We're investigating a death. Until we have more information, I cannot and will not comment," the detective answered. "Now if you'll excuse me, I'll just be goin' about my duties." He nodded toward Mack. "Sir, if you could follow me down to the station, I'll be able to question you in private."

"Is this man a suspect?" Siobhan asked.

The detective blocked the reporter's access to Mack. "Ms. Callahan, in the course of my investigation, I will be interviewing witnesses, suspects and everyone on down to the person who cleans the loos. Please, just let me do my job."

"By all that's holy, it's Deirdre Darcy!" The reporter's attention riveted on Deirdre. She yelled at the cameraman. "Are you getting this?" Then she stood beside Deirdre, facing the camera. "I'm at the Fitzpatrick Hotel in downtown Dublin. Beside me, in her bridesmaid gown, is the lovely Deirdre Darcy, being questioned about a murder that occurred in the very heart of our city. Miss Darcy, can you tell us what happened?"

Mack put a hand over the camera lens. "Back off."

"Oh, and who might you be?" Siobhan asked.

The camera man backed far enough away

Mack couldn't take a swing at him or his equipment, but he adjusted his lens, zooming in on the pair.

"Not important." He nodded to the lead detective. "Come with me." He led the way through the lobby to the business room on the other side. Once he had Deirdre and two detectives through the door, he closed it in Siobhan's face. Unfortunately, the room had glass walls and the cameraman could film all he wanted through the window.

"Since Miss Darcy can swear you were in your room during the hours between midnight and four a.m., perhaps you can tell us if you heard or saw anyone or anything out of the ordinary during that time."

"I didn't hear or see anything," Mack said. He turned to Deirdre. "Did you?"

Her heart hammered against her ribs as she recalled her encounter with the two dark-haired men in the hallway. "Detective." Deirdre touched the man's arm. "In which room did the murder occur?"

"The one immediately to the south of Mr. Magnus's."

Deirdre clutched Mack's hand, her face pale. "Sweet Jazus."

"What?" the detective leaned forward. "Did you see something?"

She pressed her knuckles to her lips. "I might have seen the murderers."

Mack's fists tightened. "When you left the

room?"

Deirdre stared into his eyes and nodded.

He brushed his knuckles on the side of her cheek. "That's why you were so frightened?"

"Yes. I bumped into one of them while he was holding a mobile phone. He dropped it and glared at me. I didn't know what he was so mad about. I dropped my purse and everything went everywhere."

"Did you break your phone?" Mack asked. "I tried to call you earlier, someone picked up but didn't say anything."

"You did? I got a call right before Fiona walked down the aisle, but when I answered, all I heard was heavy breathing." Deirdre's brows wrinkled. "Was that you?"

Mack shook his head. "Not me. I tried to call you a couple hours ago."

"I'd have been at the hair stylist with Fiona. My phone didn't ring once. Maybe it is broken. Fiona said she tried to call me all morning and I'd answer and then hang up. I never heard the calls. How could I have answered?"

"Unless you weren't the one answering." Mack's hands closed around hers. "Where is your phone now?"

"In my purse, behind the table on the dais." She turned toward the door. "I'll go get it if you want."

"No. You need to stay here," he said sharply. Then in a softer tone added, "I'd rather not disturb the wedding party any more than we have to. What does it look like?"

Deirdre gave him the description and approximately where she'd dropped it.

"Is it okay if I leave?" Mack asked.

The lead detective nodded. "Detective Doyle will escort you to the ballroom and wait for you while you gather Miss Darcy's purse. I advise you not to run."

Mack raised his hands as if in surrender. "I have nothing to hide. I didn't murder the occupant of the room beside mine."

"So ya say." Detective McLaughlin nodded to Doyle. "See to it."

Mack left the business room with Doyle in tow. He hated leaving Deirdre alone or even with the detective any longer than a moment. Especially if what he was thinking was true.

Once inside the ballroom, he avoided his brothers, slipping around the outer walls to the table at the dais. Unfortunately, his brother Sam was seated at the table, twirling a shot glass in his hand. "Hey, Mack. Where have you been?"

"Out in the lobby."

"But the party's in here. Oh wait, you're probably having your own party with the pretty model." He raised his glass. "Good for you. Ask her if she has a sister."

"I will." Mack ducked beneath the table, located the pile of clothes and purses beneath and sifted through until he found the one meeting Deirdre's description. When he rose from beneath the table, he held the purse at his side.

Sam grinned. "Nice purse."

"It's Deirdre's. She asked me to get it for her." When Mack started around Sam, his brother's hand snaked out to capture his arm. "What's wrong?"

"Nothing."

Sam shook his head. "I know when my big brother has a problem. Is it the girl?"

"No."

"Then why the heavy frown? You should be happy for Wyatt."

"I am. I just need to go." He shook off his brother's hand and hurried past him, praying he wouldn't follow and ask more questions. The fewer guests who knew about the murder, the better. At least until the wedding party had officially ended. If he had it his way, he'd send his brother Wyatt and his new bride off on their honeymoon before they got wind of what had happened.

The detective was waiting for him outside the ballroom. They were halfway across the lobby when he heard Sam call out behind him. "Mack, wait!"

Mack stopped and turned.

Sam was hurrying toward him, Ronin at his side.

"Go back to the party," Mack insisted. "I don't want Mom and Dad to get upset."

Ronin crossed his arms. "Not until we know what's going on."

Before Mack could tell him to mind his own

business, the detective beside him spoke up. "There's been a murder."

"Fuck," Mack muttered. His hopes of keeping the situation on the down-low had just been blown out the door.

"My brother wouldn't have killed anyone who didn't deserve it," Sam asserted.

"Thanks, Sam. I'm sure that statement will get me off the hook. Come on. You might as well hear what the detectives have to say."

"Are they accusing you?" Ronin hustled to keep up with Mack.

"Not yet. I had an alibi." He gave them a brief rundown of where and when the murder occurred as they reached the door to the business room and entered. He held Deirdre's purse out to her. "Show us your phone."

She dug in her purse and pulled out the cell phone, her brows furrowed. "Why are you interested in my mobile phone?"

"Look closer. Are you sure it's yours?" Mack asked.

Deirdre stared down at it, her frown deepening. She ran her finger across the screen and it asked for the lock code. "That's strange. I don't remember putting a lock on my phone."

"Are you sure that's your phone?"

"I think so. It has a nick on the back from where I dropped—" She turned it over. "What the hell?" There was no nick on it.

"When you dropped your purse and everything fell out, how close were you to where the man dropped his?"

"Right beside him. He reached for his phone at the same time. I remember because he had tattoos on his wrists and knuckles."

"Deirdre, I think you got his phone and he got yours." Mack grabbed a white handkerchief from his suit pocket, took the phone from Deirdre and handed it to the detective. "That cell phone might be key to your investigation. If the man she ran into last night is one of the murderers, you might be able to track him through that phone."

"As it is, Miss Darcy is our only witness to the man or men who committed the murder," the detective said.

Mack nodded, his jaw tightening. "That's right."

Deirdre's eyes widened. "Is that a problem?"

"Only for you, sweetheart." Mack stared into her eyes. "If you're the only one who can identify them, they might consider you a threat."

She looked from the detective to Mack and back. "Do you think they'll come after me?"

The detective's gaze shifted from Mack back to her, his lips thinning into a grim line. "Until we catch them, you're not safe, Miss Darcy."

"What are you saying?" she demanded.

The detective tucked the pad he'd been writing on into his pocket. "If they were willing to kill someone, they might be willing to kill you to keep you from identifying them in a line up."

Deirdre bit her lip. "What should I do?"

"I suggest you hire a bodyguard, or I could

arrange for a safe house, if you'd like."

"I can't leave now." Deirdre shook her head. "I have a public appearance on Monday here in Dublin. Then I'm supposed to be in Belfast on Tuesday for a talk show."

"It's your life, Miss Darcy. But if I were you, I'd lay low for a few days and let us work through the evidence."

"And put my life on hold? Just because I bumped into a potential murderer in the hallway?" She glanced at Mack. "Tell them I can't do that."

Mack sighed. "Sweetheart, you might have to, and it might be best to get out of Dublin until they find the murderers."

"Hiring a bodyguard takes time. I have no idea who to trust." She buried her face in her hands. "This is insane."

"I have an idea." Sam stepped forward. "I'm off for a week, I can be your bodyguard."

Mack backhanded him in the chest. "Bullshit. Don't you have a helicopter to fly somewhere?"

"If not Sam, why not you?" Ronin offered, his lips curling upward. "You said you wanted to find a quiet place to hole up and get some R and R. This would give you the perfect opportunity to get out of the city and find a little B-and-B to relax in."

Mack had to admit the idea had been percolating in the back of his mind since the old Irish woman on the airplane had handed him her card. He sure as hell didn't want Sam playing bodyguard to the beautiful model he'd slept with the night before.

Deirdre's face was pale, her hands trembling. When she bit on her full bottom lip, he couldn't help himself and blurted, "What about it? Can you trust me to be your bodyguard for a few days?"

Chapter Six

Deirdre sat in the seat beside Mack, for the first time in long time without her mobile phone and out of touch with her agent. After she'd called to have him cancel all her engagements for the week, she'd packed her bag and departed the hotel with Mack.

He'd left instructions with his brothers as to where they could find him and had turned off his cell phone altogether. The only time he'd use it was if they were in big trouble. Otherwise, he'd remain out of contact with them.

Mack and Deirdre had reassured Wyatt and Fiona that they'd be all right, that they should go ahead with their honeymoon to Crete. The two had reluctantly left for the airport.

Ronin and Sam would stay in Dublin for a couple extra days, keeping tabs on the investigation. If anything popped up, they'd get word to Mack by calling the B-and-B.

Once they all had their marching orders, as Mack described it, she and Mack had slipped out of the hotel wearing disguises. They'd hopped on the metro, got off at a random stop, got on at another and rode toward the train station. At one point Deirdre thought she saw a burly man with dark hair get on the back of one of the metro cars, but there were so many people cramming into every available space she couldn't be certain. When they disembarked she didn't see the burly guy and wrote it off as an overactive imagination. Their final metro stop was at the train station where they bought tickets to Limerick. Once on the train, Mack remained alert, keeping an eye out for trouble. Deirdre relaxed against him and fell asleep.

What felt like moments later but turned out to be an hour, Mack was waking her to switch trains, this one headed for Tipperary. Deirdre didn't know where they were going, but she'd put her complete faith in Mack, the man she'd met less than two days before. He could be taking her off to some quiet lonely road where he could kill her and no one would find her body for days. Or not.

In her heart, she knew he was one of the good guys. Her second biggest worry was that if she survived until they found the murderers, she might find herself entirely too dependent on one American marine. And, bloody hell, what would she do if she fell in love with him?

On the second leg of the journey, she kept distance between them, trying unsuccessfully to ignore him. As if anyone could ignore the man. He was taller than most men she knew and filled out in the most delicious way. If they weren't on a train bound for who knew where, she'd...

She'd what? Ride him again? And how would that help her in her effort not to fall in love with the marine?

Her life was too hectic, too managed by others to allow her to have a relationship. She was committed to her schedule and to people all across the world.

And in a matter of minutes, she'd had her agent cancel an entire feckin' week of appointments. Just like that.

As if a weight had lifted, she allowed herself to glance out the window for the first time since they'd left Dublin. The lush green countryside stretched out all around her. This was the Ireland she'd grown up in and loved. Fields dotted with sheep, crisscrossed with centuries-old stone fences. From the crumbling castles on hilltops and beautiful cliffs of Moor, to the seaside town of Kinsale, she loved every inch of it. Never had she felt unsafe.

Until now. If not for Mack, she'd be hiding away in some dark hotel, afraid to go outside for fear of being spotted by someone who could get word back to the men she'd bumped into in the Kilpatrick Hotel.

A shiver rippled across her body.

Mack reached out, slipped his arm around her and pulled her against his hard strength. "We get off at the next stop."

She glanced at the signs as the train pulled into the station. Cahir.

A smile curled her lips. She remembered this

little town in south Tipperary. Best known for its castle and the Swiss cottage built in the early 1800's, it was small and quaint like so many towns in Ireland. Deirdre had been there once with her mother and father when she was a little girl. They'd stayed at the hotel in town and walked to the castle where an old cannon ball was embedded in the wall from a battle centuries ago. They'd been on their way to Kinsale and had stopped to explore along the way.

Her chest tightened. She missed her parents. They'd died in a plane crash two years ago on a short jaunt to Scotland. They'd been so proud of her success as a model and had encouraged her all the way.

As she stepped down from the train, the clouds hovering over the town took that moment to release their heavy burden. Rain fell, hard and heavy.

Mack pulled an umbrella from his backpack and unfolded it over her head.

Deirdre headed for the hotel where she'd stayed with her mother and father.

As they neared a fork in the road, Mack clutched her elbow and aimed her south, walking along a narrow sidewalk that led up an incline.

"Aren't we going to stay at the hotel?" she asked.

He shook his head. "No."

"Then where are we staying?"

His lips spread in a smile. "In a castle."

"But the castle is just for tourists to visit

during the day."

He marched past Cahir Castle on their left and continued on, climbing the slight hill where another castle rose into the clouds on their right. She'd forgotten all about this castle as it hadn't been open to tourists when her parents had brought her as a child.

She read the sign on the wrought iron gate. "Castle O'Leary B-and-B. We're staying here?"

"I had a personal invitation from a very lovely woman I met on the plane. I thought we might as well take advantage of it."

"A woman?" Deirdre frowned, not certain she wanted to share Mack with anyone else.

"Yes. Her name's Kate."

They walked up the long drive and around to the front door of the small castle with one tall round turret on the south end.

"We came to Cahir when I was a little girl. I wanted to go inside this castle, but it was booked."

"Hopefully they aren't booked now."

She shot a sharp look his direction. "You didn't make a reservation?"

"I didn't want anyone to trace the call."

He knocked on the door. When no one responded, he opened it and stepped inside. "Kate O'Leary?"

"Who's askin'?" a lilting voice came from a room to the right.

"Mack Magnus."

A petite woman with short-cropped white hair emerged from a door and crossed through a sitting room crowded with antique chairs and sofas. "Mack. I didn't expect to see ya so soon. What brings you to Castle O'Leary?"

"We need a room for a couple days. Can you spare one?"

She bit her bottom lip. "Let me consult me appointment book. As of a week ago, I was booked solid. But I had a cancellation just today."

"Did you hear that Deedee? It might just be our lucky day." He hauled her up against him. "You know how I told you I was there for my brother's wedding? Well, Deedee and I decided to make it a double." He grinned. "I know, crazy, right?"

Kate's brows rose, but she didn't comment.

Mack continued, "We got married in Dublin. Deedee wanted to stay in the city, but I told her all about Castle O'Leary and she insisted on spending our honeymoon here."

"Well, isn't that a trip to the Blarney Stone?" Kate rolled her eyes. "A young couple like you two spending your honeymoon in Cahir when you could be visitin' the pubs and everything there is to see in Dublin?" The older woman snorted. "Pull me other leg, will ya?"

Mack reached out and hugged her. "It's good to see you, Kate."

"Oh now, get on out of here while I check the books." She waved toward an open dining area on a lower level. "Help yerself in the kitchen to a drink."

"I don't suppose I could have hot tea?" Mack

asked.

Kate snorted again. "As if there's any other kind. Damned Yanks, don't know a proper cuppa if it hit them in the face." She muttered all the way through the entryway back into her private rooms. "Hot tea. Ha!"

Deirdre turned to Mack, her brows rising. "Married?"

"Shh." He pressed a finger to her lips. "I didn't think she'd go for us staying in the same room unless we were. Come on, let's find that tea."

"Deedee?" She shook her head.

"Your initials. I thought I'd stick to something I might remember."

"Good thing you're not a regular spy."

"Never claimed I was. Give me a gun and a target, and I'm your man." He wandered through a swinging door into a large kitchen where a tea kettle sat on what appeared to be an antique stove. He touched the side and jerked his hand back. "Hot."

"Here, let me." Deirdre found a small teapot in a dish drainer and took a couple of teacups from a cabinet, setting them on the counter. She fished a teabag from a tin, dropped it into the teapot and draped the string over the side. Then she poured hot water from the kettle into the teapot. "Take a seat in the dining room. I'll bring this in."

"You're kind of sexy when you're all domestic."

She frowned his way. "Don't get used to it."

Mack raised his hands, a smile tugging at his lips. "Don't worry. I wouldn't dare."

"Good." She winked. "Now, get out of here before I spill this on you."

He backed out of the kitchen, the door swinging closed.

Deirdre found herself smiling over the simple pleasure of fixing tea for her man. The tea kettle clattered onto the stove as the thought solidified. He wasn't her man, and she'd damned well better remember that. Grabbing a tray from a stack, she set the teapot, cups and saucers on it and carried them it into the dining room.

"How do you like your tea?" she asked.

"I usually drink coffee, but I thought I'd try tea, since it seems to be the drink of choice in Ireland."

"It is, though I'm certain I saw coffee in Kate's pantry."

"I'm used to drinking cold tea with ice in it."

"Purely an American abomination," Deirdre commented.

She poured the tea into a cup and reached for the cream on the tray.

Mack held his hand over the cup. "I'll drink it hot, but no cream. I prefer my tea with lemon or nothing at all."

Kate stirred a drop of cream into her cup, lifted it to her lips and glanced up.

Mack studied her over the rim of his cup. "With all your travels, you haven't acquired a taste for sweet iced tea?"

She set her cup in the saucer. "Actually, I have. With a twist of lemon. It's wonderful on a hot day in the south. But in Ireland where warm days are rare, hot tea hits the spot."

"Do you find it difficult to adjust to the heat?" Mack tipped his teacup back and swallowed.

"I've done shoots on locations in the Caribbean, Texas, Arizona, in the Australian Outback and India. I find that I can adjust with the appropriate amount of sunscreen." She glanced at her pale skin. "I have the typical lily-white Irish skin and it tends to burn easily."

Mack set his cup on the saucer and reached out to trace a finger along her bare arm. "It's beautiful." His blue eyes darkened and his gaze captured hers. "All over."

Deirdre's breath caught and held at the look of hunger in his eyes. Her stomach fluttered and her core heated, making her want to drop her teacup and climb into his lap naked. Before she could get her hand to the table with her cup, footsteps sounded behind her.

"You have the luck of the Irish," Kate called out as she reentered the room. "The cancellation I had was for the turret room for the entire week. Shall I sign you up?"

"Yes, ma'am," Mack said. "And thank you. You're a lifesaver. My sweetheart would have been very disappointed if we had to go to the local hotel."

"No use going there when you can stay here." Her chest puffed out. "And I serve a traditional Irish breakfast at no extra charge."

"I remember you saying that on the plane." Mack patted his stomach. "And what is a traditional Irish breakfast?"

Deirdre nearly laughed out loud. She hadn't had a traditional Irish breakfast since the last time she'd traveled with her parents as a child.

Kate recited the menu, "Two eggs anyway you like them. Toast, tomato, beans, pudding, tea and orange juice."

"Sounds great." Mack smacked his lips. "Speaking of food, where can we go to get dinner? We haven't eaten since..." His brows dipped. "I don't think we've eaten all day."

Deirdre smiled. "And the snack you picked up in the train station doesn't count."

Kate answered, "There's a restaurant in the hotel in town, or an Italian bistro down the street from the hotel."

"If by Italian you mean pizza, I'm good for that." He pushed to his feet.

Deirdre groaned. "I haven't had pizza in two years. You can go without me."

"You're coming with me." He gathered their bags in one of his big hands. "Let's leave our things in our room and we can figure out what to eat when we walk back into town."

Kate handed them the key to their room and pointed to the turret stairs. "Climb the steps all the way to the top. I cleaned the room this morning, but once a day up those stairs is enough for these seventy-year-old knees. You'll have your own private loo as well. There are towels, shampoo and soap. Anything else, you'll have to come down here to ask. There'll be no room service."

With that, Kate left them to tidy up the dining room and kitchen, muttering as she went. "Hot tea. Ha!"

They climbed the spiral staircase to the top of the tower and faced a bright blue door. Mack stuck the old skeleton key in the lock and turned it. The lock clanked and the door opened into a miniscule room with two twin beds perpendicular to each other with barely enough room to walk between them to get to the loo beyond.

Deirdre laughed. "It's a hostel room. For students backpacking their way through Ireland."

Mack frowned at the narrow beds. "Not exactly what I had in mind."

"Perhaps Kate could see right through your lie about us being married." Deirdre shook her head and held up her left hand. "It's not as if I'm wearing a ring or anything."

"Speaking of which…" He captured her hand and held it in his. "Why isn't there a ring on your finger?"

She stared up into his eyes, her thoughts scattering. "I don't know."

"You're beautiful and loyal to your family. As far as I can tell, you're nice to people. Why hasn't some man snatched you up to be his bride?"

Her fingers curled around his and she

stiffened. "I could say the same about you."

He laughed. "I'm not beautiful, though I am loyal to my family." He lifted her hand to his lips and pressed a kiss. "As for nice to people. Not always." His lips thinned and he glanced away, a shadow darkening his countenance.

"I'll bet you're nice to the people who count." Deirdre cupped his cheek with her free hand and turned him to face her. "And you are beautiful, in a manly way. Any woman would fall all over herself to be your bride."

"Except you?" he whispered.

"That's neither here nor there." She dropped her hand from his face and forced a smile, her gaze falling to where their hands remained joined. "I have my career."

Mack nodded. "And I have mine."

Deirdre's chest tightened. "That about sums it up." She drew in a deep breath to ease the pressure on her lungs and tugged her hand free. Their brief time together was just that. Brief. No use crying over what couldn't be. "I don't know about you, but I'm starving. Even for a model. I could eat an entire pizza by myself."

"Aren't you afraid you'll gain a pound?" Mack's gaze raked her from head to toe. "Though you could stand a little more meat on your bones."

"Since we haven't eaten all day, I can spare a few calories." She moved toward the door. "Let's go."

With her hand balancing her on the stone wall, she descended the spiral staircase a little faster than was wise, an ache building at her core. Trying to tell herself it was just hunger, she knew it was a lie. The thought of the future and parting ways with the American left her feeling the kind of empty inside that no amount of food could alleviate.

"Hey, slow down." Mack caught her arm as she practically sprinted for the entrance to the castle. "Is something wrong?"

She shook her head, refusing to look at him lest he see the tears in her eyes. "I'm just really hungry."

Mack didn't believe that hunger was all that was bothering her. Something had made her sad when they'd been talking in their room. Her very expressive face was what made her so photogenic. And it betrayed her emotions every time. Rather than push for an answer she seemed unwilling to provide, he let the issue slide.

"As your bodyguard, let me go out first." Mack moved past her and shoved the heavy wooden door open, glancing around for any signs of danger before he let her pass through.

Once outside, Deirdre asked, "Do you think the killers would have followed us all the way to Cahir? We were careful not to leave a trail."

"We don't know what they are capable of. I'd rather err on the side of caution." Mack laughed. "Or as my commander would say, 'Better safe, than sorry.'"

Deirdre fell in step beside him, slipping her

hand into his. She kept up with his pace, her long legs matching his stride. The sun was setting as they neared the center of Cahir, the last rays bathing Cahir Castle in a soft orange glow. Mack made a mental note to visit the castle the next day. History had always interested him. Especially when it pertained to battles won and lost.

Past the castle and a public parking lot, the hotel sprawled on a corner to their right, with several cars parked against the curb.

Mack slowed to a stop at the corner, glancing around for any sign of trouble. "Would you prefer to eat a nice meal at the hotel? I imagine they would have a salad," Mack offered.

She shook her head. "Now that we've talked so much of pizza, my heart is set on it."

Mack squeezed her hand and turned left onto the main street running through town. A few buildings down, a sign hung over the sidewalk marking the spot for Galileo Restaurant. "That must be the Italian restaurant."

Inside the restaurant, the limited amount of seating was packed. Mack and Deirdre shared a large plank table with another couple and ordered pizza, sharing a pie between them and washing it down with mugs of beer.

They laughed and scraped cheese of each other's chins like any other young couple in love.

Mack studied her, liking the little lines appearing at the sides of her eyes when she laughed or smiled.

"Why are you staring at me?" she asked,

scrubbing at the corners of her mouth. "Do I have sauce on my face?"

"No. I just like the way your eyes light up when you smile, and the way they crinkle at the corners when you laugh."

She touched the corners. "Oh dear. Lines already? The ad companies will think I'm getting too old."

"I like them. They're a mark of your character. You know how to smile and laugh."

"I know I won't be young forever, but I hope to save more money before my looks go away."

"Are you worried?"

"No. But I don't want to worry when I can't model anymore."

"You don't plan to marry some fat-cat billionaire before your modeling days come to an end?"

She shook her head. "I'm not cut out for that life. I like things plain and simple. When I'm done modeling, I want to lounge around my house in jeans, pajamas or whatever makes me happy, making my own tea and baking cookies."

"Cookies?" He leaned his elbows on the table. "I pegged you for a scones kind of gal."

She blushed. "Sadly, I fell in love with chocolate chip cookies on my first trip to California."

"Sadly?"

"I can only indulge in one a month. I find them bloody addictive." She rubbed her belly, her hand climbing up to rest beneath her breasts.

"They are. So much so, that the mere mention of them makes me crave one." Among other addictive things, which included kissing the Irish model. He tossed Euros on the table enough to cover the food, drink and a healthy tip. Then he pushed to his feet, ready to get back to their tiny room and figure out a way to make love in a bed he was sure his feet would hang over. "If you're done here, we should head back to our fortress for the night."

"I'm ready." Her gaze met his, heat flashing in their smoky-blue depths. As they emerged onto the sidewalk, a fine mist made the night close in around them. Few people were on the street, the mist chasing them indoors to dry warmth. Mack held Deirdre's coat for her as she slipped her arms into the sleeves. Then he buttoned the front for her, starting at the bottom and working his way up, the irony of him dressing her not lost on him.

He could barely wait to get her back to Castle O'Leary and remove the white coat and every other item of her clothing. She was beautiful in whatever she wore, but even more beautiful in nothing at all.

As he finished buttoning her coat at her neck, he lifted her chin and brushed his lips across hers.

Headlights shone across her face, lighting her cheeks and eyes.

"You are beautiful."

"Thank you. For the words and for dinner— Watch out!" She glanced past him, grabbed his arms and jerked him toward the restaurant.

She fell and he landed on top of her, rolling to the side as a dark sedan bumped up on the sidewalk where they'd been standing a moment before.

Mack leaped to his feet and lunged toward the car.

Before he could reach it, tires spun on the wet pavement, gripped and the vehicle sped away into the mist.

Mack ran a few steps after it, stopping when he realized he couldn't catch up and he didn't dare leave Deirdre alone. Breathing hard, anger ripping through him, he stared after the vehicle, trying to read the license plate. It got away before he could.

A hand on his arm brought him back to the reason for him being in Cahir.

Deirdre stood beside him in street, her fingers slipping into his.

He opened his fist to clutch her hand in his. "That was too close."

"You think it was the killers?" she whispered.

"Did the vehicle swerve like the driver was drunk?"

"I couldn't tell. It all happened so fast."

"Come on, we need to get you back to the castle." As far as he was concerned, the castle would be their stronghold for the night. No one could climb the stairs without him knowing. No one would be able to run them down in a vehicle. Tomorrow, he would contact his brother Ronin and let him know of the near miss and see if Garda detectives had made any progress toward identifying and capturing the killers.

He slipped an arm around Deirdre's shoulders and hurried her through the mist, turning south toward Castle O'Leary. With a sharp eye cast in every direction, he kept a vigil on the road and any side streets they passed. Losing his focus once was one too many times. Had Deirdre not noticed the vehicle careening toward them, they could both be dead.

Some bodyguard he made. He should be concentrating on the job, not getting into the pretty model's panties.

Chapter Seven

Deirdre climbed the spiral steps to the turret room, tired, discouraged and cold. All she wanted was a hot shower, a warm bed and Mack's arms around her. "I'd like to go first in the shower."

"You got it." He took her coat from her and hung it on a hook on the back of the door. "I'm sorry about your coat."

"If it doesn't clean, I have more in my apartment in Dublin."

"I really liked this one."

She tilted her head, curious why he would like an item of her wardrobe so much. "Why?"

"You were wearing it the first time I saw you." He ran his hand over a long dark stain on the fabric. "You were flawless—every button buttoned, every fold in place, your hair tucked beneath that scarf and your eyes hidden behind those damned mirrored glasses. I thought you made the perfect ice queen." He snorted. "Boy, was I wrong."

Her body heated at the way his gaze wrapped around her like a warm embrace. She found her bag and ducked her head to keep from looking into those startling blue eyes so much like hers and yet different.

Unearthing a filmy nightgown and panties, she hurried into the loo, wondering why she even bothered with clothes. There could only be one ending to this evening. The ending where she lay naked on a narrow bed beneath Mack as he climbed between her legs and thrust his thick, hard cock deep inside her.

Her heart thumping, Deirdre closed the door to the loo and leaned her forehead against it. A smart woman would show some restraint. A smart woman would know better than to get any more involved than she already was with the man when they would soon part ways to opposite ends of the earth.

She stripped out of her soiled clothing, twisted the handles on the faucet and tried to get the shower to come on. No matter what she flipped, twisted or pulled, the water didn't divert to the showerhead.

Faced with defeat and not wanting to take a bath in the tub, she stuck her head out the door and caught Mack with his shirt off and his jeans unbuttoned. Her mouth watered like a dog staring at slab of meat.

The hard plains of his chest could have been forged in steel. The tight line of his jaw set in stone.

She gulped and almost shut the door when he glanced up and caught her staring.

"Need something?"

"I can't—" Her voice squeaked and heat rose up her chest into her cheeks. "I can't get the shower to come on."

"Let me try."

She grabbed a towel to wrap around her body before the big Yank wedged himself through the door. Barely covered, Deirdre backed as far as she could and almost tripped over the loo.

Mack entered the tight confines of the room, a smile playing at the corners of his lips. "Seems the only space available in this room is the tub."

The longer he fiddled with the faucet, the hotter Deirdre became until she could stand it no longer. By the time water sprayed from the showerhead, she'd made up her mind.

"There you go." He turned to leave.

Taking a deep breath, she spoke in her most sultry voice, the one she used for the perfume commercials. "Aren't you going to join me?"

When he glanced over his shoulder at her, she dropped the towel, stepped into the shower and lifted her face to the spray, letting the water run over her eyes and down her body, praying her invitation would be accepted. To up the ante, she cupped her breasts and leaned back to let the water hit them directly. If her ploy worked, Mack's gaze would be on them. Her nipples puckered in anticipation of Mack's hands gliding over them, tweaking the tips and then sucking them into his mouth.

Then the sound of the door closing made her heart drop into the pit of her belly. No...surely he hadn't…he wouldn't leave, would he? Afraid to open her eyes and discover the ugly truth, Deirdre squeezed them tighter to keep ready tears from falling. Mack hadn't taken her up on her offer. He'd left without even touching her once.

"Feckin' Yank. He doesn't know what he's missing," she said, her voice wobbling on a sob.

"What feckin' Yank are you talking about?" Hands wrapped around her middle and pulled her back against a naked, hard, male body.

The despair of a moment before rocketed into elation and the tears she'd held back overflowed. "Jazus, Mary and Joseph! Don't scare me like that. You took nearly a year off me life." Though her words sounded mad to her own ears, her hands smoothed across his, guiding them down to her sex as she leaned her head back on his shoulder, exposing her neck to him. "What took ya so long?"

"It was kind of hard shedding my jeans in the limited amount of space. I had to close the bathroom door to make room."

"You're a wicked man, Mack Magnus." Wicked in the best possible sense of the word.

"Damn right, I am," he agreed. "And I plan to do even wickeder things to your body." He kissed the curve of her neck and raised one hand to cup a breast in his palm. "Starting here."

"That's more like it, Yank. Have yer wicked way with me, if you will."

"I will." He tweaked her nipple into a hard point and then moved to the other. All the while,

116

the hand, threading its way through her narrow mound of curls, parted her folds and stroked the strip of flesh between.

Deirdre's legs quivered, her knees nearly buckling beneath her. It didn't take much for the marine to make her weak all over. Soon she was panting and calling out his name, thankful they were high in the tower, away from others so that she could be as loud as she wanted and embarrass or offend no one.

Mack slipped a finger into her channel and swirled it around, water mingling with her juices to make her slick and ready. One finger was joined by another and another until his thick fingers stretched her deliciously. When she could stand it no longer, she pushed his hand away and turned to face him. "Make love to me, Mack. Now."

"I thought you'd never ask." He reached for a foil packet on the edge of the tub, ripped it open and rolled it down over his full, hard staff. Then he stooped to catch the backs of her thighs in his hands and lifted her.

Deirdre wrapped her legs around him as he backed her against the wall, pressing her against cool tiles.

Then he slid into her in one long, delicious thrust.

Bracing her hands on his shoulders, Deirdre raised herself up and then lowered herself as he thrust again. The man was so big he filled her full and more. Her muscles clenched, tightening around him as he slid back out, water running down between them cooling the friction but not dampening the heat.

Mack rocked his hips, driving deeper and deeper until Deirdre threw back her head and cried. "Jasuz! That feels so feckin' good."

He covered her mouth with his, kissing her, his tongue thrusting in rhythm with his cock. When he surfaced to breathe, he whispered, "I love it when you curse."

"Why?" she asked, her breath catching as he rode her again, slamming deep inside her.

"It makes me hot," he said, his breathing coming faster. "You sound less and less the ice queen, and more the earthy Irish woman I'm getting to know and lo—like so much."

Mack closed his mouth over hers before she could ask him what he'd been about to say. If she wasn't mistaken, he'd almost blurted out the L word.

Deirdre would bet he hadn't dared use that word with any woman besides his sister. And he loved her like a brother should.

Deirdre let his slip-up pass without comment, closing her eyes, a smile curling her lips as she dragged ragged breaths into her lungs.

The faster Mack went, the thicker his cock grew. Pumping in and out of her, the friction heated and his jaw tightened. He thrust one last time and held her hips in his hand, buried as deep as he could go, his balls rubbing against her ass.

Cool water pelted them from the showerhead, barely affecting the heat between their bodies.

Several long moments later, his cock ceased throbbing and he slipped out of her, setting her on her feet in the tub. He stripped the condom off and dropped it in the waste basket.

They rinsed quickly and turned off the shower. Then with slow, gentle movements, Mack toweled Deirdre dry, caressing every inch of her body with the towel first, then his hand and finally his lips.

Deirdre returned the gesture, drying him, then exploring his body with her hands and mouth. She dropped to her knees in front of him, tongued the tip of his member. It quivered. Tonguing it again, she almost laughed at how it jerked. Then she opened her mouth and wrapped her lips around his cock.

Mack's hands curled around the back of her head, urging her closer to take more, guiding her without forcing her.

She took all of him, until his cock bumped the back of her throat. As he pulled out, her teeth softly scraped his length, wanting him to stay there. He tasted musky and sexy as hell and she liked it. Deirdre closed her hands around his naked ass and she guided him in and out, faster and faster until he yanked free.

With her hands sliding up and down his length, he ejaculated into the tub. "God that felt good. But now it's your turn."

"I don't need a turn," she protested.

"You may not think you do, but trust me, you do." He grabbed her hand and stepped out of the tub, leading her through the bathroom into the tiny bedroom. He lifted her and laid her in the middle of one of the beds. Starting at her ankles, he kissed a path up the inside of her calf, tongued the soft curve of her knee and crawled onto the bed between her legs.

She parted them, inviting him in, her tongue snaking out to dampen her very dry lips. Tingling began at her core and spread outward. If he got any closer to her special spot...

Mack tasted her skin, flicking, nipping and sucking at the insides of her thighs all the way up to where the cool castle air caressed her hot, damp pussy.

She reached between her legs and dipped a finger into her juices, swirling it around, then traced a line up to her clit.

"I love watching you play with yourself," he said. "But I want to have what you're having, and I want to be the one that makes you come."

"Well, bloody hell, do it then."

He pushed aside her hands and thrust his tongue into her pussy, fluttering the inner channel. He replaced his tongue with two of his fingers, then three, while he spread her folds wide and licked her clit in one long, wet stroke.

Her chest rose with a quickly indrawn breath. "Feck yes," she whispered. "Again."

He lapped at her clit again, sliding his tongue the length of the narrow strip in a long, sensuous glide.

She cupped his head in her hands and held

him there. "Faster."

His tongued her in short, hard flicks, touching, teasing and stroking her until she arched off the mattress, her fingers digging into his scalp, her head thrown back. "Jazus, I'm coming undone." Her insides burst into flames, the heat radiating outward to the far reaches of her body. She stiffened, her breath caught and held, and she stayed that way for a full minute before she finally took a breath and rode another wave of her release.

Mack didn't let up his assault until she collapsed against the sheets in a damp heap, her body limp. "Jeekers, Margaret and Mary, I've never been that close to heaven."

Mack burst out laughing.

She stared up at him, her brow furrowed. "What are ya laughin' about?"

"I've heard women say a lot of things, but never that I got them close heaven."

"Feckin' hell. It's true. If that wasn't heaven, I'd as soon go to hell for more of that."

Mack scooted up behind her and pulled her into his arms. They barely fit on the twin bed. If either of them rolled over, one or both of them would fall off. "I'll sleep on the other bed," he offered.

Her arms clamped down on his around her middle. "The feck ya will. You'll stay right where ya are."

"Yes, ma'am."

She softened her demand with "Please."

"That's more like it." He nuzzled her neck and relaxed behind her, his breathing growing more measured.

"You locked the door?" she asked.

"I did. Mrs. O'Leary locked the outer door to the castle behind us when we came back from town."

The poor man had to be exhausted from the past two days, staying awake on the trip into Ireland and then through the night of the murder and now.

Before long, his arms grew slack and his chest moved in deeper, slower rhythm with his breathing. Mack had fallen asleep.

Deirdre lay awake for a while, reveling in the warmth and security of Mack's arms, pushing thoughts of tomorrow from her mind. She didn't want to think about what his brothers would report. If they hadn't caught the killers, they could still be in danger. If they had, Mack's duties as her bodyguard would be over. He'd have no reason to stay with her and she'd have no reason to stay in Ireland.

With her bare body spooned against his, she didn't want to think past the next time they'd make love. And the way things were going, the night wouldn't be over before that happened again.

Mack woke once in the middle of the night. A sound had disturbed him and immediately he became alert. For a long time he lay still, listening for a repeat of the noise, but it hadn't come. Had it been a footstep on the circular staircase? Or wind finding the gaps in the stone edifices of the castle? He stayed awake, waiting.

The only sound was the soft mewling noises Deirdre made in her sleep. Perhaps she was having a bad dream where killers stalked her in the hallway of a hotel.

Mack pressed his lips to her temple and whispered reassuringly to her. "You're okay. You're with me. I'll protect you." After a moment or two, she nestled closer, a smile lifting the corners of her lips.

The longer he stared at her, the more his chest ached. Never had he wanted something or someone as badly as he wanted Deirdre. And not just for the incredible sex they shared. And not just for one, two or three nights. He could picture the lines deepening around her eyes and mouth and her pretty auburn hair streaked with gray. She'd be even more beautiful the older she grew.

He wanted to take her to Texas to the land he owned in the hill country north of San Antonio. The house he wanted to build would have wide porches all around with rocking chairs and a porch swing. They could sit on the swing, holding hands, watching the sun slip toward the horizon, turning the puffs of fluffy white clouds pink, orange and finally purple as the sky darkened and the stars lit the heavens.

Maybe they'd have a couple kids. A red-haired hellion like her mother and a precocious black-haired boy like him.

Fuck. He was screwed. In the short time he'd known Deirdre, he'd managed to fall in love with the beautiful model who had thousands of fans around the world swarming all over her when she went out in public. How could he compete with that kind of adoration? He was a jarhead, a marine, bound to serve his country. He could be deployed at a moment's notice and she'd be left behind to hold down the fort. On the flip side of that coin, she could continue to work as a model for many more years and leave him behind to travel to exotic countries and pose with handsome men.

Who was he kidding? A life with Deirdre was not in the cards for him. He wouldn't tie her down and she couldn't tie him down. Not as long as he was in the corps. He still had eight more years before he could retire. More, if he wanted to stay. Staying past twenty had never been a question for him. Until he'd met the beautiful, red-haired Irish woman. Now he was questioning everything about his life.

Damn. And it did his body and mind no good lying awake when he could be sleeping and gathering his energy for when and if someone tried to get to Deirdre. For several more minutes he lay listening for anything. When nothing happened, and no reoccurrence of the sound that had awakened him surfaced, he slowly slipped back into sleep, Deirdre cradled in his arms.

Tomorrow was another day. He'd deal with his feelings and whatever danger came his way from killers or losing his heart to a beautiful woman. As sleep claimed Mack, a heavy weight of dread settled over him, that same feeling he'd gotten before things had gone south in a Taliban village raid on his last rotation to Afghanistan.

Chapter Eight

Deirdre slipped from Mack's arms as the sun edged through the curtains hanging in the turret window. She had to shake her arms several times to get the blood flowing properly, having slept in the same position all night long. Grabbing clothes, her makeup kit and curling iron, she barricaded herself in the loo, determined to put on a presentable face in front of the marine who'd volunteered to protect her and had unwittingly stolen her heart.

As she'd lain in his arms last night, she'd contemplated her life as a model in high fashion, walking various runways or posing for pictures in national ad campaigns for which she was still in high demand. She should be glad about it, only she wasn't. She couldn't go anywhere without having photos snapped of her and whomever she was with. She couldn't be free to run around town in jeans and a T-shirt, or skip makeup for even a day for fear of ending up on the cover of some feckin' sleaze rag. And forget lying on a sandy beach anywhere without some paparazzi swarming her for an impromptu interview. Her life was not her own, and she was tired of it.

Her parents had been happily married and had doted on her as their only child. Deirdre had sworn to marry someone who made her as happy as her parents had been and to have three or four children. No only child for her. It was too damned lonely.

Had the circumstances been different, she would not now be with Mack. She'd be at a public appearance in Dublin and on the road shortly after to be on the set of a talk show in Belfast the next day. From there she was due to fly out to the Bahamas for a swimsuit shoot, and she lost track after that.

Some life. The more she traveled, the more makeup it took to cover the ravages of sleepless nights and jetlag. She had an apartment in Dublin, but it had never really felt like home. Since her parents' deaths and the subsequent sale of their house in south Dublin, she hadn't had a place to call home. Being with Mack, his brothers, sister and Fiona reminded her of what having a family meant.

Families meant being surrounded by people who loved you. And when they weren't around, it wouldn't take long for them to be there for you when you needed them. She could see the love Mack had for his brothers and sister and their love for him in the way they kidded around and the way they came to his assistance when he needed them. They'd even included Fiona in their family since Wyatt loved her.

Deirdre dressed quickly, pulling on a pair of designer jeans, a white button-up blouse and an Aran wool cardigan. After brushing the tangles out of her unruly mop of hair, she dabbed a light foundation on her skin to protect it from the sun's rays and applied a dusting of powder. She swept mascara across her long eyelashes and passed on the eye shadow. The curling iron had heated enough and she applied it to her hair in long, steady strokes, straightening the kinks out of her bed-hair, leaving it in long, full, bouncing waves.

Fiona was lucky to be a part of the Magnus clan.

The image in the mirror clouded behind a wash of tears. Deirdre blinked to clear her vision, only it caused more cloudiness. When a tear slipped from the corner of her eye, she knew she was in more trouble than she cared to admit. After only a few short days, she'd fallen for the American, his big, bulky muscles and his protectiveness. Worse still, she'd fallen in love with the idea of a big family and found herself envying her cousin's marriage.

If it was just Mack, would she feel the same about him?

Another tear slipped from the corner of her eye and her shoulders sagged.

Yes. She had fallen for the marine despite all her warnings to herself. Feeling the need to get away from Mack and her feelings for him, she unplugged the iron, packed away her makeup and opened the door to the bedroom where he was sleeping.

Only he wasn't there.

A rush of panic assailed her senses and she ran to the other door, opening on the spiral staircase that led down to the second and first floor of the castle. She leaned over the railing. Though she couldn't see the bottom, she could hear Mack's voice.

She backed away from the stairs, pressing a hand to her chest in an attempt to slow her racing pulse. In that second she thought he'd gone, she'd felt like she'd had her heart ripped out of her. Her reaction was utterly ridiculous. Soon he'd be gone from her life for good and she'd be on her own again. She'd better get used to it.

Slipping her feet into her shoes, she grabbed her purse and headed down the stairs to find Mack talking with the other guests of the castle in the sitting room. The spacious dining area was empty except for Kate, bustling in and out setting the tables and positioning condiments.

When she had all the tables set, she waved toward the dining room. "Breakfast will be served momentarily. Please come take a seat at the tables."

Three older couples and a four college-aged kids settled in, claiming seats.

Mack waited for Deirdre to join him before entering the dining area.

She glanced up at him. His face was clean, though heavily stubbled, and his hair was neatly combed back from his forehead.

"I didn't mean to take so long getting ready. Where did you wash up?" she asked.

"There was a guest powder room on this floor. I thought I'd let you take your time." He winked. "All worth it if you ask me. You're beautiful as always." He squeezed her hand, shot a glance toward the guests and turned back to steal a kiss.

Deirdre leaned into him, but the kiss ended all too soon.

"We should sit. Kate appears to run a tight ship." He waved her ahead of him.

Her cheeks burning at the way she'd practically fallen all over him, and angry at herself for her reaction, Deirdre straightened her shoulders and led the way to the remaining table. Mack pulled her chair out for her and she sat.

Kate served each table with plates of the traditional Irish breakfast as she'd advertised the night before. Deirdre and Mack were last to be served, sitting silently awaiting their turn.

Mack dug in as soon as Kate served their plates.

Deirdre ate one of the eggs and a slice of toast, not very hungry but determined not to let Mack know it was because of him.

In the time it took for Deirdre to choke down the egg and toast, Mack had cleaned his plate of everything but the pudding.

He poked the disks with his fork and cut into one of them, lifting it to his mouth for a bite. He grimaced. "It looked like sausage, but it doesn't taste like sausage."

"Because it's pudding."

"Back in Texas, pudding is soft, creamy and sweet."

Deirdre smiled. "You're not in Texas, cowboy."

He grinned. "No, I'm not. And it's pretty damned cool to be eating breakfast in a castle. The men in my unit wouldn't believe this place. Remind me to snap some pictures."

As Kate cleared the plates from the tables, the telephone in the sitting room rang. The castle owner excused herself to answer.

A minute later, she returned. "Mr. Magnus, it's for you."

A knot lodged in Deirdre's throat as Mack rose to his feet.

"I'm coming with you," she said, grabbing her purse.

He didn't argue. Instead, he helped her out of her chair.

Together they left the dining room and found the telephone on a table in the sitting room.

Mack lifted the old fashioned receiver. "Hello." He waited then repeated, "Hello?" His brow furrowed and his hand tightened around the receiver. A second later, he slammed the receiver down. Immediately he picked it up, dug a piece of paper out of his wallet and dialed the number on it.

After a moment, he spoke. "We've been found." He hung up and grabbed her hand. "Time to leave."

"Who was it?" Deirdre asked.

"No one." Mack pulled her along behind him, heading for the stairs to the turret.

Struggling to keep up with him as he dodged around settees and wing-backed chairs, she asked, "Then why are we leaving?"

He paused at the bottom of the spiral staircase. "No one knows we're here."

Her eyes rounded and her heart plummeted to the bottom of her belly. "Except your brothers."

"And now someone else." He pointed to the stairs. "I'm staying here. Go up and gather whatever you absolutely have to have and get back down here ASAP."

She patted her purse and shook her head. "I have my purse. I don't need anything else."

"Then we leave now."

Deirdre followed Mack back through the dining room. "What about Kate?"

"We're going on a walking tour of Cahir, if she asks. That's all she needs to know."

"If we're leaving, shouldn't we go out the front door?" Deirdre pointed to the entrance.

"There's a door through the kitchen that leads to the outer wall of the castle grounds. It's a shortcut to the train station." Mack grabbed a stack of plates and handed them to Deirdre. "Take these." He lifted another stack and headed for the kitchen.

Kate backed through the swinging doors as they reached it. "You don't have to clean up after yourselves. That's part of the package."

"We don't mind, do we, Deedee?" he said with a big, fat, fake smile.

"Not at all," she replied.

Mack eased past the older woman. "We'll leave the last table for you, Kate." Then he pushed through the swinging door and Deirdre followed. They ditched the stack of dishes on the counter beside the sink and hurried out the backdoor into a cloudy, gray Irish day.

"Which way?" Deirdre whispered, her head swiveling around, her pulse pounding. If the killers had found them, they'd be waiting for them to make a move. They might even be watching all entrances to the castle and the surrounding grounds.

"I'd feel better if I had a weapon," Mack lamented.

"Me too." Deirdre ran alongside him, glad she'd worn flats and blue jeans instead of the dress she'd packed. "If they know we're here, won't they expect us to go to the train station?"

"The first train leaving in the morning departs in exactly ten minutes. If we made a clean getaway, it'll take a few minutes before they realize we're gone. Hopefully that'll give us time to board the train and take off from the station before they can get there. But we have to get there before the train leaves."

Deirdre ran faster. Though she exercised on a regular basis, she used treadmills and elliptical trainers. She wasn't used to running all out and her lungs were struggling to provide enough oxygen to the rest of her system.

By the time they arrived at the station, her chest burned and she was wheezing with every breath she took. Mack fed Euros into the ticket machine and punched the buttons that produced two tickets to Dublin. Tickets in hand, they raced for the correct platform position to board. The train doors were open and all passengers had boarded. Deirdre and Mack leaped onto the train and hurried forward through the cars. Mack insisted on Deirdre leading the way while he brought up the rear.

At the juncture between cars, Mack paused and glanced behind them. "Fuck!" He shoved her through and ducked in behind her. "Stay low and keep moving."

"What's happening?"

"Was one of the guys you ran into in the hotel, tall, really broad, with swarthy skin and heavy black eyebrows?"

Deirdre leaned against the train's wall. "Yes."

"He's about to step on board with another man. Shorter, and maybe a scar on his face."

"Jazus, Mary and Joseph! That's them."

Mack pushed her through to the next car. "Find a door and get off the train."

As she emerged into the next car, she ran for the doors and jumped off. The doors closed automatically behind her. She turned in time to see Mack trying to pry the doors open.

Deirdre shouted, "No!" and banged her palms

against the doors as the train moved forward.

Farther down the platform, two burly, black-haired men stepped back from the train and turned toward her.

Her feet remained stuck to the concrete. She couldn't move and she was back in the nightmare all over again as Mack and the train slid away from the station as if in slow motion.

Then adrenaline kicked in and she tore her feet loose from the imaginary shackles holding her to the platform. She had a twenty-meter head start on the men. If she could get out of the station and hide in the twisting, narrow streets, she might survive.

Deirdre ran for the exit, taking the stairs upward two at a time. Footsteps pounded behind her, closing the distance between them.

A sob rose up her throat, but she didn't have time to feel sorry for herself. She swallowed it and ran across the street, dodging a passing lorry and ducking between two of buildings.

A shout rose up behind her. She didn't stop to glance back but kept running. If she wanted to live, she had to keep going.

Mack tried to get through the sliding train door by jamming his fingers into the gap. But the door closed firmly, trapping his fingers. As he fought to free them, the train pulled slowly away from the station and Deirdre. Through the window in the door, he saw the two men who'd boarded the train on the platform several cars down from Deirdre.

"Damn!" He pulled hard, but his fingers were stuck. Bracing his foot on the door, he yanked hard enough he finally freed his hand, the fingers throbbing as blood rushed back into the digits. Then he hunkered down and slammed his shoulder into the door. It didn't open.

Until the train cleared the small town it wouldn't gain much speed. If he wanted to get out in time to help Deirdre, he had to do it fast. He ran to one of the windows, lowered it from the top. It was barely enough room to let air in, but he had to try. He climbed onto the seat and shoved his head through, then his shoulders. Pushing against the back of the seat, he wedged himself through the narrow opening and fell to the platform below, slamming his shoulder against the concrete just as the train picked up speed.

By the time he got out, Deirdre was gone and all he saw was the back of one of the dark-haired men, racing for the train station exit.

His pulse hammering through his veins and adrenaline blocking the pain in his fingers and shoulder, he charged down the platform to the exit.

Once outside, he slowed, caught sight of the man and sped up.

The guy was the smaller of the two men and dressed in a suit. He appeared to be carrying something in his hand as he ran across the street and slipped between two buildings.

Mack ran out into the street and was nearly struck by a car. The driver honked, but Mack ran on, ignoring the shouts, his focus on catching the man carrying what looked like a gun, before he found Deirdre.

Ducking between the buildings, he emerged in an alley behind them. The narrow road through the alley was empty. A flash of black caught his attention as a man slipped through the gap between more buildings backing up to the alley.

Mack followed, his heart in his throat, praying he wouldn't be too late.

The gap between the buildings emptied onto a road leading to the main highway running through town. The men were nearly half a football field away when Mack saw them again. They were headed for the massive stone walls of Cahir Castle. Ahead of them, he saw a flash of red hair as Deirdre dove through the wooden doors of the castle.

He only had to get to the bad guys before they got to Deirdre. Unarmed and so far behind, he feared he wouldn't make it in time. Sucking in a deep breath, he increased his speed.

Failure was not an option.

He crossed the two-lane highway and ran along a bridge and through the gate. The broad wooden door stood open. He hurried through and paused briefly to listen for shouts or sounds of footsteps.

For a moment, he heard nothing. Then the soft sound of feet disturbing gravel made him turn right into the main portion of the castle buildings. He hurried through the arched passages and beneath a jagged-toothed portcullis into an open area. He stopped in the shadows, listening again. A movement to his left caught his attention. Slipping along the base of a large rectangular building, he eased up to a door and peered around the edge. The larger of the two men stood in a hallway, peering into a room. After only a second, the man moved to the next room. In his hand was a pistol, his finger resting on the trigger.

If Mack had any doubt this man was not a tourist, the gun settled it.

As short as the hallway was, it wouldn't take the big guy long to clear the floor and start up the stairs.

Mack eased into the building and snuck up on the big man as he turned toward a stone staircase. When Mack was close enough, he barreled into the man's shoulder. The big guy pitched sideways and his head slammed into the ancient stone wall with a dull thud.

He slipped to the ground, out cold. Quickly, Mack removed the man's tie from around his neck, rolled the man onto his belly and jerked his arms up behind him. Using the tie, he bound the man's wrists together. If he woke up in time, he wouldn't be of any assistance to the smaller guy. Mack grabbed his gun from where he'd dropped it on the ground.

A scream echoed through the walls of the castle.

Mack abandoned the unconscious man and ran for the door. Another scream sent him running toward the building at the far south corner of the grounds. When he burst through the doorway, he found Deirdre in the clutches of the smaller man. He held her by her glorious red hair, tugging back viciously while holding a gun to her temple.

"Mack!" she cried. "Jasuz, Mary and Joseph! I thought you were gone."

His lips twitched despite the gravity of the situation. Deirdre made every word she spoke sound like music.

"Stay back, or I'll kill her!" the Traveler shouted.

"You're going to die either way," Mack warned him.

"Perhaps, but not before yer girl dies." He jammed the barrel into the side of Deirdre's head so hard she winced.

"Get out, Mack," Deirdre begged. "I'll be okay."

He knew better than to let the bad guy take her. He'd kill her as soon as he had safe passage out of the castle. Mack refused to let him by. "Give it up. Too many people have seen you now. If you kill her, there will only be more who can identify you as the murderer you are."

"Are you deaf? Move or the girl dies."

"You'll have to kill me first, because if you shoot her, I'll be on you so fast you won't know what hit you. And you won't like how much pain I'll inflict before I let you die." He worked his way closer. "Oh, and in case you think you're covered, your buddy is out cold and tied up like the pig he is. He won't be coming to help you."

The man's brows narrowed and he glanced past Mack as if to verify. His gaze returned to Mack and he yanked harder on Deirdre's hair.

She squeaked and stood on her toes to ease the strain on her roots.

Mack banked on the man shooting him first. As soon as the hand holding the gun shifted forward, Mack dove to the right.

A shot rang out and pain zipped through his side.

Chapter Nine

Deirdre's heart jumped when the gun went off beside her. She'd seen the barrel turn right before the man pulled the trigger. Rage blasted through her that this man would shoot Mack.

She cocked her elbow and twisted hard, ignoring the pain in her scalp. She'd lose every hair on her head before she let Mack die. Her elbow landed dead center in the man's solar plexus.

He jerked, loosened his grip on her hair and Deirdre sprang free.

When he turned the gun on her, she didn't have time to react.

And she didn't have to.

Mack lurched to his feet and plowed into the man's side, knocking him over. The gun went off, the bullet going wide of its target.

The men rolled on the ground until Mack got the upper hand and pinned the bad guy beneath him.

The shooter angled the gun toward Mack's face.

Deirdre's breath caught and held as she rushed forward and kicked the gun so hard it flew out of the man's grip and clattered against a stone wall ten feet away.

Her attacker grabbed Mack's throat and squeezed.

His face turning red, Mack punched the man

in the face until he went limp, blood squirting out of his nose.

Rolling to the side, Mack stared up at Deirdre. "Thanks." For a moment he lay there, breathing in enough air to fill his lungs, then he struggled to sit up and yanked the man's tie from around his throat.

Deirdre helped roll her attacker over and held his wrists together as Mack tied them securely.

When he was done, the marine dropped to the ground, pressing his hand into his side. "Have someone call the police and an ambulance." He lay on his back on the ground and immediately passed out.

That's when Deirdre spotted the blood staining Mack's shirt and pooling on the stones beneath him.

Her stomach lurched as she scrambled to her feet and ran for help.

The man in the tourist shop was talking to a uniformed member of the Garda and pointing in Deirdre's direction.

"Please help me," she cried. "Call for an ambulance, now!" She spun and ran back to the courtyard where she'd left Mack. Her hands trembled as she shook off her sweater and yanked open her shirt, stripping it from her shoulders. She tore the hem with her teeth and ripped it up the middle, folding one side into a tight square.

Kneeling beside Mack, she laid the square of fabric over the wound and pressed firmly to staunch the bleeding. "Bloody hell, ya can't die on me now. Ya feckin' better live. I'm not done with ya."

Mack's lips curled up and his eyes blinked open then closed again. "Anyone ever tell you that you're beautiful when you're mad?"

"Feckin' right, I'm mad. Pullin' an idiot stunt like that. Darin' the fool to shoot ya."

"It worked, didn't it?"

Keeping a firm hand on his wound, she cupped his cheek with the other. "Jeekers, Mary and Margaret. You could have been killed." She glanced down at his wound. "You might still die if someone doesn't get the feckin' ambulance here!" The last half of the sentence she yelled over her shoulder, angry that she couldn't do more. If she moved her hand, he'd bleed to death.

"Aren't you Deirdre Darcy?" The uniformed member of the Garda appeared beside her.

"Don't go there if ya know what's good for ya," she warned.

"It's just that I'm a huge fan." He glanced down at Mack's pale face and wiped the smile from his lips. "Want me to take over?"

"Feck no!" she stated. "I'll only turn him over to proper medical staff." She nodded to the man tied up on the ground. "You should be takin' care of that one there. He tried to kill my man."

The Garda rolled the man over. "A Traveler, is he?"

"Yes. And if you'll contact the Dublin Garda, you'll discover that he committed a murder two nights ago." Deirdre glanced around. "He had an accomplice around here somewhere. Mack said he'd put him out of commission."

"I'd say this one isn't doin' anyone harm the way his is now." The Garda left the man on the ground and went in search of the other. He emerged from a nearby building as a siren's wail entered the gate of the castle.

Soon two emergency medical technicians arrived, carrying a stretcher. They set it down alongside Mack. "We'll take over from here."

One of the men pushed her hand aside, lifted the square of fabric and checked the wound, while the other checked Mack's vital signs and fixed an oxygen mask over his face.

More Garda arrived as the two attackers regained consciousness. The uniformed men helped them to their feet and marched them out of the castle.

A single member of the Garda remained behind with Deirdre and the EMS. He gathered her sweater from the ground. "Miss Darcy, ya might want to wear this, or you'll catch yer death in this mist."

She hadn't even noticed the falling mist as it mingled with tears trickling down her cheeks, or the fact she'd been half-naked as men came into and left the castle grounds. Shoving her arms into the sweater, she buttoned it over her bra and hugged herself, the cold seeping through to her bones.

"Is he going to be okay?" she whispered.

"His pulse is strong and his blood pressure is

steady."

"Yes, but is he going to be okay?" she persisted.

"He should be, God willin'." The paramedics rolled him onto the stretcher and carried him out to the waiting ambulance.

"I'm going with him," Deirdre stated. It wasn't a question and the ambulance personnel didn't argue. Instead, they handed her up into the back of the ambulance. She perched on a seat out of their way, her focus on Mack all the way to the hospital in Clonmel, thirteen kilometers away from Cahir.

As they unloaded Mack at the emergency entrance, she waited beside the ambulance.

The medical personnel wheeled him in on a stretcher. Deirdre walked beside him, holding his hand.

Mack's eyes blinked open. "Where are we?" he said into the mask covering his mouth.

Deirdre smiled down at him. "At the hospital."

"I must have fallen asleep. Someone kept me awake last night."

"These kind gentlemen are going to take you to surgery." She hated to let go of his hand, but she wasn't allowed any farther into the hospital than she was.

"Will you be here when I come out?" he asked.

"Yes."

He closed his eyes. "Good. I have something

I want to say."

"It can wait."

The hospital staff wheeled him through a door marked authorized personnel only, and Mack disappeared.

What felt like hours later but by the clock had only been about forty-five minutes, a doctor emerged with blood on his white smock. "Are you a relative of Mr. Magnus?"

"No. But I'm the only one he's got here."

"He's lost a lot of blood, but we got the bullet and stopped the bleeding. He should be fine in a couple days."

A flood of relief made her legs wobble. "Thank you."

When the doctor turned to leave, she laid a hand on his arm. "When can I see him?"

"When he's awake. The nurses are settling him into a room. It shouldn't be long."

"Thank you." Deirdre paced the waiting room, counting the minutes until she could see for herself that Mack was okay.

A ruckus in the hallway made her turn.

"Where is he?" a deep, male voice demanded.

"Sir, Miss Darcy is in the waiting room, perhaps she can give you an update while I find the physician."

Her heart warming, Deirdre hurried out into the hallway.

Sam, Ronin, Wyatt, Abby and Fiona were

headed her way.

She fell into their arms, the tears she'd held back flowing freely.

Fiona and Abby hugged her tight. Sam, Ronin and Wyatt gathered around and joined the hug.

Wyatt broke away first. "What happened? The last thing we knew was that you two were making a break from Castle O'Leary. We got here as fast as we could. Mom and Dad waited in Dublin in case they could be of assistance to the Garda. They are on their way now."

Deirdre gave them the short version of their escape from the B-and-B and the fiasco on the train. She ended with her attempt to lose the killers on the grounds of Cahir Castle, only for Mack to end up shot in the belly. "The doctor assures me he'll be all right. He's in recovery now. Hopefully, they'll let us see him soon."

Sam shook his head. "I'd have paid good money to see the showdown in the castle. Trust Mack to make it a new page in the history book."

"I'm just glad he survived." Deirdre collapsed into a chair and buried her face in her hands. "It's all my fault."

Abby sat on one side of Deirdre.

Fiona sat in the chair on the other side and tugged her hands away from her face. "How's this your fault? You didn't plan on bumping into killers after they'd offed one of their own."

Ronin dropped to his haunches beside her. "And you couldn't have stopped Mack from volunteering to be your bodyguard. He'd have done it regardless."

Sam nodded. "I saw how he looked at you. The man has it bad."

Deirdre sniffed and glanced up at Sam. "Bad?"

"I'd say. He's pretty well stuck on you."

"How could he be...stuck on me? He's only known me three days. One when he volunteered to be my bodyguard."

Abby smiled. "Didn't Mack tell you? Our parents fell in love on their first date."

Wyatt added, "I fell in love with Fiona the first time I saw her and pulled her dripping wet out of the San Antonio River."

Fiona smiled and reached for Wyatt's hand. "It took some convincing for me to believe him." Her smile broadened. "And here we are. Married."

Deirdre sat up straighter. "Jeekers! You're missin' your honeymoon!"

Wyatt patted Fiona's hand. "We agreed we couldn't enjoy it not knowing whether you two were going to be okay. As soon as Mack's out of the woods, we're flying out of here to Crete for some R-and-R on a sandy beach."

"Excuse me." The young lady dressed similarly to the one who'd talked to them in the hallway stood in the doorway to the waiting room. "Are you Mack Magnus's family?"

Everyone, even Deirdre answered with a resounding "Yes!"

"He's awake and bellowing for someone named Deirdre." When Deirdre stepped forward, the woman's eyes widened and she clapped a hand to her mouth. "Jeekers! You're the Deirdre he's callin' for?"

Deirdre nodded. "I think so."

The woman flapped her hand to cool her reddened cheeks. "My sister is never goin' to believe this. Come with me."

"Hey, what about us? We're his family too," Sam said.

"Well then, what's keepin' ya?" the young woman snapped, tempering her words with a smile. "Move, move, move. I have work to do, ya know."

The six of them crowded into Mack's room where he lay on the bed, his eyes closed, some of the color back in his cheeks.

Ronin whispered, "I thought they said he was awake."

"He is, doofus." Sam elbowed Ronin in the ribs. "He's just playin' us for sympathy."

"How could I be asleep with all of you stomping into my room like a herd of elephants?" Mack opened his eyes and grinned. "Damned glad you could make it."

"We came as soon as you called. It just takes time to get here from Cashel."

Deirdre frowned. "I thought you were stayin' in Dublin."

"We figured on seeing a little of the Irish countryside while we were here, and that closer was better if Mack needed backup." Sam tipped his head toward Mack. "Which it appears he did."

Mack reached for Deirdre's hand. "I had backup. You should have seen Deirdre slam an elbow in the gunman's gut."

Sam's brows rose. "She did that?" He let out a long sigh. "I'm in love."

"Back off," Mack said with a little more force.

"The way I see it, she's not spoken for and therefore fair game." Sam slipped an arm around Deirdre's waist. "What do you say to you and me?"

Deirdre laughed and shook her head. She'd had a talk with Sam. He'd told her that he loved to tease his brother and that he knew her feelings for Mack and that his flirting wasn't going anywhere.

Apparently Mack wasn't certain his brother was only teasing. He pushed to a sitting position, wincing. "Goddamn it, Sam."

Sam dropped his arm, the smile slipping from his face. "Mack, you shouldn't move around so soon after surgery. You gotta give yourself time to heal."

"Then get your stinkin' paws off my girl."

Deirdre's pulse quickened at Mack's proprietary words. Though secretly thrilled, she couldn't let him throw out words like that without securing her agreement first. "Your girl?" She propped a fist on her hip. "Since when am I anyone's property but my own?"

"Whoa, Mack, you should know better than to piss off a redhead," Wyatt said.

"After last night, I thought—" Mack collapsed against the bed and grimaced. "Fuck! That hurts."

Deirdre softened and laid her hand on his arm. "Listen to your brothers. You need to heal. We can talk later."

Mack reached for her hand, capturing it in his. "I don't want to wait until later." He glared at his brothers. "Can a guy get a little privacy?"

Wyatt laughed and popped a salute. "Leaving." He grabbed Sam's arm and jerked him toward the door. "Let him have some time to grovel."

"We're brothers," Sam protested. "We're supposed to give him hell."

"Another time." Ronin took Sam's other arm and between him and Wyatt they dragged Sam out of the room, followed by Abby.

Fiona lagged behind, her brow furrowed. "You two be smart about this. Life's too short to lose out on love because you think you haven't known each other long enough or won't be around each other enough. Trust me. That's what I thought, until I met Wyatt. If you want something bad enough, you find a way." With that, she left the room and closed the door behind her.

Mack tugged her closer, until Deirdre had to either sit on the bed or lie on top of him. Because of his injury, she scooted onto the bed beside him. "You really should get some rest. A gunshot wound is nothing to be feckin' with."

Mack's mouth curved. "I love it when your uptown polish slips."

"I'll have ya know, I worked hard for my polish. For nearly ten years, I rarely said a curse word. Then you showed up and the killers and...and...I fell in love and now my life is fecked to hell." She sagged. "What am I goin' ta do?"

"Marry me," Mack blurted. "Holy shit. I said that out loud, didn't I?"

"Damn sure did." Deirdre's heart fluttered, but she didn't let her hopes rise too high. "You shouldn't say things like that when yer fecked up on pain killers."

"I'm not fecked—I didn't let them dope me up and my side is killing me. I wanted my head to be clear when I saw you again."

"Why? So you can say any fool thing that comes to your head, whether you mean it or not?" She tried to get off the bed, but his hand on her arm kept there. "What do ya want from me? I have my life, you have yours. We're not suited."

"You're half-right."

"About which part?"

"About each of us having our own lives. But you're very wrong about us not being suited for each other." He pulled her closer until she had to plant her hands on either side of his head to keep from toppling over on him and reinjuring his wound.

"We don't live in the same country," she said.

"You're talking geography. I'm talking chemistry. Different sciences." He captured her chin in his hand and leaned up to brush a kiss across her lips.

When he lay back on the pillow, she sucked her bottom lip between her teeth, electric currents rippling through her at his touch.

Mack's brows rose, challenging her. "Chemistry."

Her brows furrowed. "You can't build a life out of chemistry. You have to be together. We wouldn't be. Because of our commitments, we'd go days, even months apart."

"Now, you're talking quantity." He leaned up again and kissed her harder, this time he slipped his tongue between her teeth and caressed the length of hers.

Her thoughts scrambled and heat built at her core.

"I'm talking quality." He cupped her cheek. "The time we will have together will be that much better. And when we get to a point in our careers where we've had enough, we can build a life together full-time. Anywhere you want."

"I've only known you three days," she said, her heart already lost to the love in his eyes.

"It only took a moment for me."

"What if it takes me longer to know for sure?" she whispered.

"Take all the time you need. I'll wait." He cupped her cheek. "Just say you'll be mine someday."

She stared at him, her head telling her to run as far and as fast as she could, her heart shouting for her to stay, telling her she'd finally come home. Tears welled in her eyes, one slipping down her cheek.

He brushed it away with his thumb. "I love

you, Deirdre Darcy."

Another tear trailed down her cheek. "I think I love you too."

Mack cringed and smiled. "Not exactly what I was looking for, but it'll do for now. My challenge is to convince you to take a chance with me."

She slid her hand over his chest. "I'm afraid."

He captured her hand. "Me too. But I'm not giving up."

Chapter Ten

Mack stood beside Deirdre at the door to Castle O'Leary.

"Kate, come away with me, darlin'." Sam hugged the castle owner and swung her off her feet. "I swear my undying love for my bonnie Irish lass."

Kate smacked at his arms, her cheeks cherry red, her eyes shining. "You're far too young for me and your Irish accent needs improvin'."

Sam gave her a loud kiss on her cheek and set her away from him. "Thanks for putting up with the Magnus clan during Mack's recuperation."

"'Tis my pleasure. Now, leave me be to go back to me work." She hurried into the castle, her face still flushed.

It had been a week since Mack had been released from the hospital. Abby, Sam and Ronin had managed to con Kate into letting them stay at the castle while Fiona and Wyatt had flown off to Crete to finally have their honeymoon. Mack's parents had come for a few days and then gone on their long-awaited sightseeing tour of the Emerald Isle.

Mack had agreed to stay on in Cahir for another week to be sure he was fit before traveling. Then he was going to Venice with Deirdre where she was scheduled to shoot an entire spread in one of the fashion magazines. With a month off, he figured a week in Venice and the following week in Texas would give Deirdre time to get used to the idea of them being together forever.

He hoped that in Venice she'd consent to be his wife. Hampered by his injury, their lovemaking had been pretty tame lately. But by the time they made it to Venice, he'd bump it up a notch and seal the deal. She wouldn't be able to let him go.

Or at least he hoped.

Abby, Sam and Ronin each hugged him hard and clapped him on the back, careful not to touch his side.

"Don't go messin' with those Traveler men again. I can't always come bail you out," Ronin said.

"I didn't need you the first time." Mack drew Deirdre against his good side. "I have my secret weapon to protect me."

"Yeah, we see that." Sam kissed Deirdre on the cheek. "Remember, I love you too. If you decide to ditch my gimpy brother, I'm your man."

Mack shoved him away. "How many times do I have to tell you, she's not that into you?"

Deirdre laughed. "Sam, there's a woman out there who's just right for you."

Mack nodded. "All you have to do is be smart enough to recognize her when she comes along."

"Easy for you to say. You got the best girl."

"Damn right I did." Mack pressed a kiss to the top of Deirdre's auburn hair and then turned to Sam. "You have another two weeks of leave. Where are you headed?"

"I've always wanted to go to Italy. All your talk of Venice has me curious. Maybe I'll play forward scout and clear the bad guys before you two land."

"Be sure to find us then. We'll have dinner on one of the canals." Mack shook his brother's hand, and Sam slid behind the wheel of the rental car.

Mack faced Ronin. "You're going back to the States?"

"Yup. Got word this morning from my commander. He wants me back ASAP to fly some super secret mission." He winked at Deirdre.

Mack nodded. Because they were all in the military, every time they parted, he refused to say goodbye. The danger involved in their careers left them with no guarantees. He never knew if he'd see them again and he didn't want to jinx them. "I'll see you later then."

"Later." Ronin bumped fists with Mack and climbed into the rental car.

Abby hugged Mack. "If you make a trip to the Ukraine, be sure to come see me. I miss my brothers something fierce."

"You bet. But it goes both ways. We'd love to see you move back to Texas."

"And what embassy would I work at there?" She snorted. "I didn't major in foreign relations to live forever in Texas."

Mack kissed her forehead. "I had to try."

Abby hugged Deirdre. "Thanks for taking care of my big brother. You're already like a sister to us."

"Not to me," Mack amended.

"Next time I see you, you have to show me how to do a smoky eye with my makeup." Abby squeezed Deirdre's hands.

Deirdre nodded, tears in her eyes. "I will."

A moment later, with Abby ensconced in the backseat, the car pulled through the castle gates and drove away.

"I miss them already," Deirdre said, "and they're not even my family yet."

Mack grinned. "Yet? Does this mean you're giving in?"

Deirdre poked a finger into his chest. "Don't push me, Yank. When I'm ready, I'll tell ya, and not a moment sooner."

"Then let's go make use of our turret. I have a whole lot of convincing to do."

"You've already ripped your stitches once."

He slipped his hand down over her bottom and pinched her. "I'll make a deal with you. You can do all the work and I can lay back and enjoy it."

She smiled, her eyelids drooping, low and sexy. "I have a better idea. One that will keep you from rippin' a stitch." With a wink, she grabbed his hand and led him into the castle.

"We're goin' upstairs, Kate!" Mack called out.

"We won't be down until breakfast."

"Bloody hell, be off with ya, and keep the yellin' down, will ya?" Kate shouted back. "I have other guests, ya know."

Mack followed Deirdre up the winding staircase to the tiny room at the top. Rare sun shone through the windows as Deirdre stopped in the bright rays and stripped her clothes, letting her bra fall from her fingers to the floor.

"Now, your turn," she said, and proceeded to undress him, taking her sweet time, trailing lips across his skin like butterfly kisses. His body trembled with a surge of lust unparalleled to anything he'd ever felt with any other woman but Deirdre.

When he was as naked as she was, he reached for her.

She scooted backward, shaking her head. "No, no, no. Not yet. We aren't going to do anything to disturb your injury. Now lie down on the bed."

Mack complied, stretching out on the mattress, the expectation of what was to come making his cock as hard as a poker.

"Ready, are ya?" she asked, her gaze traveling low over his body.

"Always. With you."

Deirdre bent over him and kissed his lips, pushing her tongue past his teeth to twist with his. When he tried to pull her down on him she broke the kiss.

"This is the part where I do some of the work

and you do some of the work, but we both get off satisfied."

"Well, hurry it up, woman. I'm about to explode with anticipation."

Deirdre moved her lips across his chin and down to his chest, capturing one of his nipples between her teeth and nipping gently. Gradually inching her way down his body, she stopped to run her hands across his engorged cock.

"I know I'm liking this, but how is it getting you where I want you to go?"

"I'm gettin' to it," she said and wrapped her lips around his dick, sucking him into her mouth.

He surged upward, the muscles in his belly tightening and tugging against his stitches. "Ouch."

She backed off him and said, "Lie down and let me do the work."

"Yes, ma'am."

When she came down on him again, he let her, forcing his body to lie still when every instinct was to thrust upward into her warm, wet mouth.

Deirdre moved over him, planting one knee on the edge of the bed and lifting the other over his head, positioning her lovely lady parts over his face.

"Now you're talking." He cupped her bottom and pulled her down on him until he could flick her clit with his tongue.

She sank lower and purred. "Mmmm, yeah." Her mouth closed over his cock as he lapped at her pussy, alternating between tonguing her clit and thrusting into her juices.

Deirdre was right, he didn't have to work hard to get off with her. And from how wet she was already, it wouldn't be long before... He tapped the strip of flesh, flicking, teasing and nibbling.

Her back arched and she grew rigid, the edges of her teeth scraping his shaft.

Oh yeah, she was close.

Sliding his fingers into her pussy at the same time as he ravaged her clit, he hit the spot and her hips jerked, her body shaking with the force of her release, cream sliding from her channel.

Her mouth moved over his cock, powering up and down until he couldn't see straight and sensations pushed him to the very edge. He held on, refusing to come in her mouth. Instead, he grabbed her ass. "Protection," he said through gritted teeth.

She reached for one of the foil packets they kept handy on the nightstand and tore it open, sliding it down over his cock. Then she left the bed and mounted him, sheathing him in her drenched channel. Rocking up and down, she rode him until he could take no more and he rocketed over the top. He held her hips in his hands, pushing her down over him, his cock buried as deeply inside her as he could get it, throbbing and pulsing against her moist heat.

When he could string two thoughts together, he helped ease her to the mattress on his good side and held her for a long time.

She nestled her cheek against his chest and

sighed. "Okay."

"Okay what?"

"If you'll have me, I'm yours." She slid a hand across his skin, careful not to disturb his wound. "Jazus, Mack, I can't help it. I'm falling head over heels in love with you."

He pulled her into his arms and kissed her. "Then stop fighting it and surrender."

About the Author

ELLE JAMES also writing as MYLA JACKSON is a *New York Times* and *USA Today* Bestselling author of books including cowboys, intrigues and paranormal adventures that keep her readers on the edges of their seats. With over eighty works in a variety of sub-genres and lengths she has published with Harlequin, Samhain, Ellora's Cave, Kensington, Cleis Press, and Avon. When she's not at her computer, she's traveling, snow skiing, boating, or riding her ATV, dreaming up new stories.

Learn more about Elle James at
www.ellejames.com

Or visit her alter ego Myla Jackson at
www.mylajackson.com

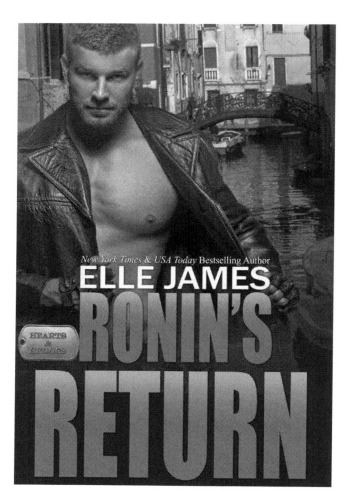

New York Times & USA Today Bestselling Author

ELLE JAMES

HEARTS

RONIN'S
RETURN

RONIN'S RETURN

HEARTS & HEROES
BOOK 3

New York Times & *USA Today*
Bestselling Author

ELLE JAMES

COMING SOON

19056576R00097

Printed in Poland
by Amazon Fulfillment
Poland Sp. z o.o., Wrocław